KINGDOM *of* MONKEYS

KINGDOM ═*of*═ MONKEYS

STORIES BY

Adam Lewis Schroeder

RAINCOAST BOOKS

Vancouver

Raincoast Books acknowledges the ongoing support of the Canada Council; the British Columbia Ministry of Small Business, Tourism and Culture through the B.C. Arts Council; and the Government of Canada through the Book Publishing Industry Development Program (BPIDP).

First published in 2001 by

Raincoast Books
9050 Shaughnessy Street
Vancouver, B.C.
V6P 6E5
(604) 323-7100

www.raincoast.com

Edited by Joy Gugeler
Typeset by Bamboo & Silk Design Inc.
Cover design by Les Smith
Cover painting by Earl & Nazima Kowall/CORBIS

1 2 3 4 5 6 7 8 9 10

Canadian Cataloguing in Publication Data

Schroeder, Adam Lewis, 1972-
    Kingdom of monkeys

 ISBN 1-55192-404-8

  I. Title.
PS8587.C49K46 2001   C813'.6   C2001-910182-1
PR9199.3.S268K46 2001

Printed and bound in Canada

This is all for Nicole

"The people of each country get more like the people of every other country. They have no character, no beauty, no ideals, no culture — nothing, nothing."

Her husband reached over and patted her hand. "You're right. You're right," he said smiling. "Everything's getting gray, and it'll be grayer. But some places'll withstand the malady longer than you think."

— Paul Bowles,
The Sheltering Sky

CONTENTS

SEVEN YEARS WITH WALLACE

Ali and Wallace stood together at the rail, looking down at the grey water of Singapore and the sampan bumping against the prow of their steamer. One of the men in the sampan peered up at them from under his hat and, as always, Ali smiled down.

The captain of the steamer approached the rail, carrying an empty tumbler.

Mr. Wallace turned and shook hands with him. "It's been a lovely voyage," Wallace said. "I prefer these big ships."

"What's your destination?" asked the captain. He was Dutch, but his English was excellent after years of dealing with the bureaucrats of Malaya. He was forever running his tongue across his cracked lower lip. "Perhaps up to Malacca?"

"No," said Wallace. "I am finished. I am going home to England."

"Finished? You mean sacked?" The captain gazed out at the roofs of the shop-houses, then at Wallace's bearded face.

"Oh no, certainly not. I was never employed by any one person in particular, only myself. Though certainly I *was* dependent on buyers in England to keep the money coming in. I collect specimens of natural history, you see. Surely you saw my boxes down below. Those reflect only what I have collected in the past few months, in Sumatra. I have had dozens more sent on, nearly two hundred, I should think. At least I hope so!"

One of the Javanese crew joined them and the captain told him in Dutch that if he wanted to shut the engine down it was all right and that coal couldn't be had for free besides. Then he went back to gazing at Wallace. If the gin hadn't run out he would not have had to come out on deck and endure this conversation. "I saw your cargo," the captain said, "but I thought it was clothes. You like to look correct, I think."

"Well, this suit I only bought in Surabaya and let me tell you, up until then I had but two shirts and my trousers were in shreds. In Sumatra I had to find proper cases for my collections ... no, it has not been easy, I should say."

The captain nodded and wiped at his neck with his sleeve. He wore trousers and a shirt that was missing most of its buttons, both once white, but now speckled with grease and rust.

"How long have you been east?" asked Wallace.

"Thirteen years."

"Eight for me."

"Your boy, he's worked for you the entire time?" asked the captain. "Let me tell you, he's robbed you blind. Every one of them is alike. What is he, Ambonese?"

"Oh no, he's a Dyak, from Borneo, but perhaps you do not know the famous Ali, my friend, or you would not dream of speaking that way. Ali!" called Wallace.

The boy leaned an elbow on the rail and shaded his eyes to look at them. He wore a blue sarong and an old shirt, possibly one of Wallace's.

"How long have we been together, lad?" asked Wallace.

"Since 1855, sir."

The captain thought this sounded rehearsed.

"There. Seven years," said Wallace, with a grin. "And the most extraordinary discoveries I owe to him. Incredible specimens. You would think God was delusional when he fashioned them, you surely would. Birds with such plumes on their heads as you can't imagine. I would venture to say that God did not make them *at all*, but that they made themselves and the next variety along as well. That's my way of thinking."

"I'll see about your luggage," said the captain. He started down the passage, the tumbler still in his hand. He knew from experience that Wallace would gladly go on talking for days, despite the delights of Singapore spread before him — real white women only steps away. It was the same with all Englishmen, they thought it rude to do otherwise, and those who have spent years away from other white men are only *more* obsessed with propriety. They were forever bowing and scraping, these Englishmen, thinking him a man of some importance in the Indies because he'd been trusted with a new iron steamer. In truth it was the quiet of the old ships he longed for, those without clattering engines, only the creak of rope, the flutter of sails, the silent tilt of bottle and glass on his table. After thirteen years he hated the Javanese and other Dutchmen besides. He loved only the one thing.

Ali held the bottom of the rope ladder as Wallace climbed down and the two men with oars sat ready in the rear of the sampan, nearly hidden behind packing cases. Chimes clattered in the stern. A breeze across the water blew Wallace's beard against his cheek, so that several times he had to brush it down and hold the ladder with only one hand. The sampan gave a sudden heave and bumped against the steamer and Ali cried out. The tip of one finger had been crushed between the two boats; blood welled under the nail and trickled down his hand. Wallace stepped down into the swaying boat.

"Did something happen?" he asked.

Ali smiled and gripped the finger in his good hand.

"Right, let's get to shore," Wallace said to the men. "Town awaits."

A crewman stepped to the rail of the steamer and emptied a barrel into the water as the sampan pulled away. Wallace stared with fascination at a dead rat that bobbed to the surface. It was only a common rat, though, *Rattus norvegicus*; had it a furred tail or an iridescent coat, some uncommon trait, he would surely have leaned over and plucked it from the sea.

He estimated his collection after eight years in the Indies at one hundred thousand specimens, with very little repetition of species, save those he knew Europe would always have an appetite for: the orangutan and the myriad varieties of bird of paradise that had kept him criss-crossing the islands off New Guinea. Horrible days in little boats, with only he and Ali and one or two natives as crew, waiting out a windless spell with the next island just out of sight, looking at each other, looking at the water, trying to keep calm. Wallace had occupied himself then by wondering whether the next island would be bereft of animal life or so thick with undiscovered species, crawling and climbing and fluttering about him, that he might work the rest of his career there, playing host to other scientists, perhaps to the Geographical Society. Surely, he had thought, if he spent so many years in one place, even old Darwin could be coerced into a visit.

He had never found one enchanted place, though — only the ten thousand islands of the archipelago, overpoweringly rich in fauna, collectively, but visited over many years and in precarious little boats. He had only the strength now for one last trip in a little boat, the sampan to the dock. He'd have no more *praus* or canoes or rowboats, travelling at the mercy of the tropical weather and the Sulu pirates. That was no way for a man to live. The only place for him now was England.

One hundred thousand specimens in eight years. If three years were more than one thousand days, eight years would be three thousand days, so he'd collected more than three hundred specimens each day. Now, suddenly, nothing — he'd taken nothing since he'd left Sumatra two days before — and nothing ever again. Once home he would remember these eight years, polishing each like a gem.

The sampan slowly pulled its way between trading junks at anchor, their crews stretched out on their wooden roofs, catching the cooling afternoon breeze as it swept over their chests and shaved heads. The day was overcast and humid, but the wind skipped off Sumatra — the monsoon was not far off. The Chinese lolled on the sturdy junks and gossiped while pots of tea were served. A basket of vegetables was passed from one boat to another and a shirt flew off a clothesline into the water. Its owner groped for it with a boat hook and the other men laughed.

Ali watched as they drifted by. The language of these Chinese sailors meant nothing to him. They were yet another community, one of a hundred in the archipelago, which he simply floated past.

Months before, he had met a pair of fellow Dyaks working the port at Batavia. They had told him that there were a few others in Singapore, if he was going that way, headhunters ridding the seas of pirates for the English East India Company. They had found this arrangement most amusing, for there were no pirates more fierce than the Dyaks themselves, the Sea-Dyaks. They had laughed then and one had told a crude joke, but Ali had not understood it. He had not spoken his own language since Wallace had taken him from Borneo.

"Sir?" said Ali.

"What is it?" asked Wallace. He was brushing something off the arm of his coat; it seemed to be fish scales.

"Will we be very occupied in town?"

"I believe," said Wallace, "that the ship departs for England in two days. We will investigate, of course. I may have acquaintances to call on, you understand, if they are still in the east and not on leave. You know, as often as not, a man is not where you left him. With luck we can leave these things at the shipping office and will not have to bother ourselves with ferrying them to the hotel. Have you seen these rickshaws the Chinese have?"

"Pulled by a man," said Ali. "In Kuching we saw them."

"Oh, of course," said Wallace.

Ali dipped his hand into the water, thinking it might cool his poor finger, but the sea was warm. He sucked at the blood instead and watched the fish rush beneath the surface.

"Are there many others like me in England?" asked Ali.

Wallace did not care for riding in small boats. He glared at another sampan as it veered rather close off their stern.

"Thank you, no," Wallace said. The emaciated rickshaw men crowded them, shouting out names of hotels, banks, public offices, plantations, jostling each other and running their hands over Wallace's shoulders as though admiring his coat. Ali stayed close behind as they made their way off the boardwalk and onto the dirt streets. The men from the sampan were hauling the trunks up onto the pier, looping ropes through the cases' leather handles. Three rickshaw drivers stood by, cousins of the sampan men. They would follow Wallace to the shipping agent with his

14

collection of hornbills, pheasants, monkeys, lemurs, curious butterflies, emerald-tinted beetles and numerous other specimens that he had extinguished, dried and tacked into place while in Sumatra. Wallace did not concern himself with the unloading. He had seen the natives' habits where such things were concerned and found that he only got in the way when he endeavoured to direct them. Instead he and Ali wound their way through the markets along the waterfront, followed doggedly by a handful of rickshaw men. It was worth their trouble to persevere; Europeans never knew how much to pay.

Singapore was rife with voices, like a forest full of birds. Arabs shouted and held bangles out to Wallace; Japanese held up writing-paper and string; Malays sang as they sat gutting fish; Mohammedan women pushed past in tawny burkas, haggling with the vendors, baskets under their arms; excited Chinese children held the hands of their mothers, who yelled for their own mothers, shuffling behind; a Hokkien shopkeeper stood in a doorway, shouting angrily at the neighbouring merchant.

Ali looked everywhere, but there were no Dyaks.

Wallace turned back to him and pointed out a sign written in Portuguese. "Before I know it," Wallace said happily, "every signboard will be in English."

They had lost the rickshaw men. A Bengali squatted against a building, razors clattering in his hand, inviting Wallace to have his beard shaved. Piles of rubbish that had earlier been swept under market tables now tumbled back underfoot, so that bones, rinds and faeces were crushed into a sort of carpet Ali padded over with bare feet. Wallace started to feel weak and an ominous feeling came over him. His malaria had come and gone so often he knew the signs only too well.

A poorly-dressed European man came up and took Wallace's

arm. "Good day," he said. He might have been German. "You speak English?"

"I do," said Wallace.

"You have enthusiasm," the man said quietly, "for gentle ladies?"

Without a word, Wallace removed the man's hand and he and Ali pushed on. Soon the marketplace narrowed and they found themselves in a neighbourhood of stilt-houses, built over another section of waterfront. Beyond the houses stood jungle.

"We have lost ourselves somewhat," said Wallace. "And not for the first time."

The vendors called to them again as they worked their way back through the tumult. The glow of the sea was visible far ahead. Wallace hummed a little. Ali recognized the song as the one Wallace sang on the open ocean to bolster their spirits, but Ali had never been told its name. They passed a stall where chicken roasted over open coals.

"Only a handful of meals left to me before I start home," said Wallace. "What do you suppose I should have?"

"Yams," said Ali. He smiled slyly.

"Oh no," said Wallace, with a chuckle. "Certainly not those."

The ship for England would be leaving in the morning. Wallace hesitated for a moment when the agent asked if he intended to be on board and gazed out the open door of the office and down the stairway to the street. He'd hoped to spend the next day rambling inland, perhaps have a look at the tiger traps near the Jesuit mission.

Then something in his chest began to rattle and he had to lean against the desk. He coughed for a full minute before his breath returned. He wondered what was the matter with him; a cough like that had nothing to do with malaria. Doubtless with every new species he'd handled he had swallowed a handful of diseases.

"I certainly will be aboard tomorrow," Wallace said. His eyes were still watering.

The agent opened his ledger and began to write.

Ali stood away from them, studying the framed timetable on the wall. There was a steamer for Borneo every Friday, but he told himself that England was also a fine place. In fact, every person not already in England wished that they were. A moth fluttered beneath the glass.

"I've had some interesting clients come through lately," said the agent.

"Oh, who was that?" asked Wallace, leaning heavily against the wall. A Malay man copying letters cast him a sympathetic look.

"The Oxford Cricket Club," said the agent, "on their way to Australia. First time a club's made the trip."

"Wonderful."

"Good-looking men. Couple of them had really terrific beards. You'd have fit right in, Mr. Wallace."

"You think I would have?" He forced a smile.

"Oh, I know you would!"

Wallace was disappointed with the Royalist Hotel. The tea in the lobby was cold and the desk clerk was Chinese. Of course, he was still in Asia; Europeans were all managers at one post or another. But still, with the Royalist he would have expected a retired corporal out of India or even a cockney with side-whiskers — anything to demonstrate that, of all the hotels in all the outposts, this one was *English*. But he was not in England yet. He handed the teacup to one of the hotel boys and walked to the desk, Ali padding along behind. More boys stood swishing fans.

"I am afraid I have not written ahead. A room for Wallace and servant."

"Please sign," said the clerk, pushing forward the register. He wore a jacket and starched collar.

Wallace dipped the pen. "Alfred Russel Wallace, Naturalist," he wrote and then, "accompanied by Ali." He turned and winked at Ali, who was watching over his elbow.

"The hotel requests," said the clerk, leaning forward very slightly, "that the gentleman's servant be clad in better attire."

"I beg your pardon?"

"His clothes are not clean," said the clerk. "Perhaps … perhaps he could be outfitted like a gentleman if you — "

"Really, like a gentleman? We have spent years sleeping on beaches, my man, praying that another snake was not going to drop onto our heads. This lad was given a … a human skull to play with as a child. We have been in utter wilderness nearly every day of the past seven years and now I wonder if he would like to sleep in a proper bed. He is not the Duke of York, granted, but I would dare say neither are you!"

"In both sleeping out of doors and within a hotel, sir," said the clerk, "one may entertain certain expectations."

Wallace looked down at Ali.

"You could do with a new suit of clothes, couldn't you? In any case, we'll not be tricked out of our room."

The clerk watched as the Englishman strode away through the lobby, the boys with fans scattering before him and the poor servant trotting behind. Here was Singapore in a nutshell.

The clerk undid the clasp on his collar and set it down on the desk. One of the boys took the teapot away and the rest sat down cross-legged on the floor. The doorman would signal if the general manager or a guest was on his way in.

The general manager was having the clerk read Marlowe,

because, he said, the clerks at every other hotel were reading Shakespeare. The clerk didn't enjoy reading Marlowe, though, because the words were too blurred; as he grew older his eyesight grew worse. The general manager wouldn't allow him to wear spectacles. He said that a Chinaman in spectacles looked every inch a trained ape.

Ali knew that Mr. Roland the tailor was a terrible man, though Wallace did not seem to notice. The tailor shoved Ali around. He put a pin right into his arm.

"Lively smell the lad has," Mr. Roland said to Wallace. "Not much for baths, are they? Never seen one buy a cake of soap, have you?"

Wallace sat in a teak chair in the far corner, his head propped on his fist.

"They have always lived near water," said Wallace. "This far west I have not found that they have any smell at all."

"It's no wonder they have an odour," said Mr. Roland, taking the pins out of his mouth, "swimming in that filth."

The edge of the carpet was furrowed with tiny bites; Wallace contemplated what sort of insect might have been at work. He thought of the millipedes and beetles tacked into place in his collections, the crates he would have to unpack and finish classifying. That in itself could take years, and then to get all his findings on paper. But, for those necessary years, he would at last be alone with his thoughts, in the cool and quiet of England.

For years he'd been toying with titles for the book: *The Land of the Orangutan and Bird of Paradise*, or *A Scientific Narrative*, or *Studies of Man and Nature*. Yet none held the power of Darwin's *The Origin of Species*. None ever could. Such a title spoke of … everything!

A trickle of sweat ran behind his ear.

"And the trousers, in velvet as well? A white cotton might be more comfortable but you want the best, I presume. Mr. Fullerton was in not long ago to have something done up in velvet."

"Fine," said Wallace. He gazed upward, watching the fan move across the ceiling; it was rigged to a cable through the wall and pulled, presumably, by a coolie on the street. The canvas sheet resembled a sail. Soon there would be no more sinking boats, no more sails sitting idle. He thought of the excellent sleep he would have that night at the Royalist, on beautifully white sheets, smelling so clean. He would sink into the soft bed as though to his death.

A woman passed the window, a white woman, followed by a boy carrying her parasol. Wallace watched the clean line curve up from her corset to her bosom, that long swoop that was so wholly feminine. He shifted in his chair to watch her, but she passed and was gone.

Once he had sat in a rocking boat and watched a volcano erupt off Mindanao. The horizon had filled with ash. He had wondered where the ash might travel on the wind, what species of bird it might choke, how his work might be affected. Then he had inexplicably thought of a woman's bosom and the perfect line of her corset, how a woman perfumed herself in a dark room. After a time his crew had asked where he intended the boat to go.

"I'll have my man start on the shirt, Mr. Wallace," the tailor was saying. "Do you prefer the low collar, or perhaps, if we have velvet for the suit, you'd like a ruffled shirt? It's been selling well here for a number of years. What do you prefer?"

"Ruffles," said Wallace.

Ali very much liked the ruffled shirt. He stood on a raised platform, looking into the mirror.

"He doesn't look like a Kling anymore, now does he?" said Mr. Roland. "He looks like a proper lad who's dressed up to look like a Kling."

"Klings are from India," said Wallace. "And this boy is from Borneo. He was a very good assistant to me, at harder work than you have ever done."

"There aren't any real Klings in Singapore, anyway," said Mr. Roland. "They're all half-English and half-Chinese and the Chinese all act like Malays and on and on. In my letters from home, they ask me to send them joss-sticks now. Joss-sticks! Like I was the Chung-King God of Rice! I feel sorry for these Klings of yours. No man of any race is a proper man of his own race any longer. Now you see what's missing on your lad? Shoes are what he needs. His feet look as wide as a couple of spades."

In the end Wallace chose not to buy shoes for Ali. They both knew it would have been a waste of money. Ali reminded himself, though, that in England nearly everyone would be wearing them.

Ali walked through the dark, past the shop-house porches and silent men smoking long pipes. The docks stretched nearly the whole length of Singapore, but the hotel boys had said to go in this direction. Wallace had fallen asleep over his supper.

The evening was cool but, wearing the new suit of clothes, sweat ran down Ali's back and dripped from his fingers. He was accustomed to blending into his surroundings — though in the Papuan islands he had clearly been an outsider, with lighter skin and finer features, still, far less an outsider than Wallace — and there was no reason he couldn't blend in here but for the suit of clothes. The trousers were too long and already the cuffs were matted with dirt.

He walked past shops and food vendors. People bumped into

him and walked on without pause. Everyone was Chinese, walking with their families or chatting in front of the tea houses. Paper signs fluttered above them. Children played with metal toys on the pavement. A woman with a pole across her shoulder sold soup from the pots dangling at either end.

There were no Dyaks here, and for good reason. On such an evening, they would have dancing and stories, drinking palm wine called *arrak*, in a house with a fire on the floor. The whole village would be together. The smell of smoke would touch everything and the *arrak* would be powerful. Its taste filtered unbidden into Ali's mouth.

In the Aru islands all the men drank *arrak*, but Wallace did not let him. Wallace knew nothing about being a Dyak. At his age Ali should have been a warrior, been allowed to take an enemy's head to display with all the other heads his family had ever claimed. But he was not a warrior; he collected birds. When he was small he and his friends had played at war, sharpening sticks and howling and tackling each other into the river. That was as close as he had come. He remembered how happy his aunt had looked when his cousin had gone to fight, and how the other women had paid her their respects.

His father had been dead for a long time and, though every woman laboured in the field as she did, his mother felt that because she was a widow her children were poor and looked down on by other families. When Wallace came through the village and asked for a porter, his mother volunteered Ali. She saw the silver ornaments that Wallace carried and imagined her son returning with handfuls of them. But he and Wallace went overland instead, across another river, and spent several months gathering orangutan skins. Ali called them *mias* then, he did not know the word "orangutan," and Wallace had no beard at all.

In their first week together, Wallace shot an orangutan seven times, but still it did not fall from the tree. They stood on the forest floor scratching their heads. After it had not moved for several days, Wallace thought it safe for Ali to climb up and get it. Scrambling far up into the canopy, he found it was a male, with a meaty face like a full moon and insects crawling out of its empty eyes and slack mouth. All of its flesh had been eaten away, so that when Ali tipped it out of the tree it fell to the ground and broke open. Wallace found eighteen new species of insect inside the orangutan, and he complimented Ali, saying he was "a most rare specimen."

So Ali did not return home. He saw many other Dyaks as he and Wallace travelled around Borneo, but they were not his family and after a while he and Wallace left Borneo entirely. Ali did not question this because he knew he was a rare specimen.

At the end of the crowded street stood a tall brick building, with lamps illuminating a sign over the door that read EAST INDIA COMPANY EST.1600. A cripple was sweeping the steps. Ali waited for him to shuffle away and then tried the handle on the great mahogany door. It opened and he squeezed inside, stepping onto the cool marble floor. There were no lights inside, but a big white man with a thick moustache was coming toward him with keys jingling in one hand and a candle in the other.

"Out! You, out!" he barked. He was English.

Ali lowered his head reverentially. He had been practicing what to say.

"Sir," he said, "I'm looking for the Dyak people, do you know of them?"

"Well, who are you, then?" The candle cast a white light under the Englishman's jaw and just above his eyes.

"I am assistant to Mr. Wallace, the naturalist."

"Kyaks? I don't know them. What are they?"

"They are from Borneo. I am also from Borneo."

"You don't look it."

"They have hair grown very long and a red cloth on the head." He did not think of his own people in these terms — in fact, this description was from Wallace's journal, with which he had first learned to read. "They wear a blue cloth about the loins. They are very strong." He squeezed his own arm to illustrate and was disappointed to feel the cloying velvet.

The Englishman cocked his head to study Ali.

"You're a more clever lad than usual. Have you been in England?"

"Not yet, sir. Perhaps I go tomorrow."

"Very good. The Kyaks, you say. They work for the Company? Go to the back, straight toward the water. You'll come across our warehouses and such. Some people are living in there — might be who you want. And when you get to England, tell them Matthew Brown said good morning."

"I am grateful," said Ali.

The lane through the warehouses was not lit. He ran his hand along a stone wall, feeling his way. Someone approached and Ali crouched in a doorway. It was a sailor with a bundle over his shoulder.

In the jungle Ali had nearly always been alone, spending days scouting for birds with his gun, meeting Wallace again in the evening, but in the towns they had always been together. They had stayed away from saloons; they had spent evenings at the homes of government officials, English or Dutch.

He wondered if Wallace had woken up and if he wondered where his boy was.

He crept from one building to the next, listening for his brother Dyaks, but listening for *what* exactly he wasn't sure. He remembered the melodies of their songs but not the words; the more he thought, the more vague his memory became, until all he could remember was the song Wallace always sang. He would sing the last line the loudest. It went "Till we have built Jeruuuusalem in England's green and pleasant laaand." That was when the night was black, the waves were coming over the boat and they knew a reef lay ahead. Wallace had been brave.

Ali heard laughter and men talking. He stood and waited at the door, his head bowed. There were Dyaks inside, he was sure of it.

For a year he had thought of nothing else. But instead of sliding the door open, he toyed with the ruffles on his shirt while his heart pounded. His fingertip throbbed. He held it against his palm like a tiny jewel of pain.

The door opened with a screech, sliding sideways, and a man his own height leaned out, coughing and hiccuping. He spat a few times, then noticed Ali's splayed feet and looked up into his face.

"I am a friend," Ali said, in the Dyak language.

The man did not respond, but stood looking at him with a lopsided frown. Too late, Ali noticed his short hair and his flowered sarong, instead of blue and white stripes — perhaps he was not Dyak at all.

Another man thrust his head out, looking identical but with a red handprint on his chest. He glared at Ali. "What?" he said, in English.

"What do you want?" asked the first man, in Dyak. "What is your name?"

"Ali. I have not been home for seven years."

"We have not been home for a month!" said the second happily. "They made us cut our hair!"

"Come inside," said the first. He put an arm around Ali, who choked a little at the smell of *arrak* coming off them.

"Look at his clothes," said the second.

It was more like a cave than a building; it had no windows and fires were burning in two corners. Half-naked men crouched in groups, passing flasks of liquor. One man lay groaning on the floor.

"A brother!" said the second man, then shouted something too quickly for Ali to follow. The men all got to their feet. They crowded around him, touching his velvet coat, stroking it with the backs of their hands. It was strange for Ali to be with so many men his own height. One tugged at the shirt ruffles, but the others pulled him away. They were all giggling, their faces hot. Ali's hair was tousled and someone studied his scalp.

"Seven years," they said.

"With the white men," said the first man. He used *putih*, the Malay word for white. "All alone with white men."

"You work with us," said a young man. "Come tomorrow. We will all go home."

"Are you strong?" someone else asked.

They began to clap their hands, everyone falling into a rhythm and backing away to make a circle around Ali. One man stepped up and knocked into his arm, hard, then kicked him several times in the leg. They were wrestling. Ali had forgotten. He ran at the man and grabbed him around the waist, pulling him down to the floor. Everyone yelled and the clapping intensified. Then his opponent was laughing, so it seemed the match was over.

Ali stood up, ready for the next challenge, but the men sat down in their groups once more. One man turned from the fire and vomited, the liquid hot and white.

Ali stood near the door. The first man pushed past him and spat into the alley again.

"You work for the whites?" Ali asked.

"We work hard," said the man. "It never stops."

"You fight pirates?"

26

"No, no. We carry things from the boats, rice and guns and coffee. We all want to go home."

"Who fights the pirates then?" said Ali.

"The pirates are all dead. Shot by the whites."

The man looked Ali square in the face, then spat on his trouser leg.

There was shouting behind them; his wrestling opponent was motioning Ali back to the fire. The man who had vomited dropped the flask, spilling *arrak* into the flames, and the men leapt to their feet in anger.

Ali stepped into the lane and walked away.

There were certain streets where only Europeans went, though often their servants went with them. But the clubs were for whites only, the shops exclusive, the hotels run by families who'd been in Singapore at least two generations. Gas lights had been put in on a few corners, policemen — Malays, mind you — walked their beats and many of the great English banking firms had offices facing one another. If not for the heat under your collar and the clouds of mosquitoes coming off the swamp, you might be in London, in the City. Fifty feet of cobblestones had been put in.

Thousands of insects circled the haloes of gas light. Wallace stepped from one doorway to the next, peering into restaurants.

"A fine evening," he said to a doorman.

He rounded a corner and was disappointed to realize he'd entered a Chinese neighbourhood and had still not found what he sought. The European quarter was only so big and he had covered all of it. He turned to retrace his steps and found her standing right behind him, leaning coyly on a folded parasol. He kept his head.

"A fine evening," he said.

"Are you English?" she asked.

"Yes."

"I am Belgian."

"I do not mind," he said.

They walked for a while into the Chinese neighbourhood, side by side but a few feet apart. She had her parasol over her shoulder. Wallace watched her closely; she was not the woman he'd seen at Roland's. The line of her corset was perfect, though, and the way her head tilted prettily as she looked at him filled his heart. She walked confidently past the shops.

They turned and went up a flight of stairs. An older woman wearing a wide hat greeted them at the door. They came into a carpeted hallway and for the first time the Belgian girl took his hand. They went through a door and sat on a divan. From another room Wallace heard a man howling.

"I will guess," she said and studied his face. She touched his beard. "Four years."

"I have been east eight years."

"Since you have been with a woman?"

"Ten years."

"You are sweating." She took out a handkerchief and wiped her hands. "You are very wet."

Sweat ran in rivers down his face and he leaned forward onto his knees. The man who had been howling moaned for a moment and then chuckled. The house went quiet. She tried to keep Wallace from falling to the floor.

"I so much want to be home," he said.

"There is another girl, who is English. Should I get her?"

"I want to be home."

The woman with the hat came in but she looked blurry to Wallace; she might have been a beetle standing upright. He slid off the divan to the floor.

"What's the matter with him?"

"He wants an English girl."

"Where's Bessie?"

"She is out."

They helped him into the hallway and back down the stairs. With his heavy arm around her neck, the Belgian girl planned where she would go next. The evening was just beginning. She could stay close to the good hotels. People treated you well in Singapore, they knew what a hardship it was for a girl to come all this way. Besides, it was better for the English and German and Swedish boys if there were white girls around, rather than having to go to the natives. The native girls were filthy and did not look after themselves, that's what she told everyone. Under their sarongs they crawled with disease.

At the bottom of the stairs, Wallace let go of her and took a few faltering steps up the alley. The woman in the hat tut-tutted.

"He wants to go home to England, you see?" said the Belgian girl, laughing a little. "He is on his way now. He has nearly made it."

There was a rickshaw at the corner and Wallace fell into it.

"The Royalist Hotel," he said to the man and though Wallace was twisted in the seat he felt himself drift into sleep. "It's not a proper hotel, is it? Have you seen it?"

As they went under the gas light a handful of moths knocked against the seat and Wallace tried feebly to brush them away.

Ali left the lobby and stood in front of the hotel. Without Wallace there the clerk would not let him into the room. Ali's eyes were drawn up to the sky: a black sea with a net of constellations cast over it, and bats and insects whirring in patterns of their own. Soon he would be in England and the stars would be different.

He inspected his finger: it was purplish now and much too big. The nail was loose and the skin radiated a queasy heat. He tried not to think about it, but he couldn't help remembering natives they had seen with legs and arms oozing infection. In England, he reminded himself, there were wonderful doctors. It would be so simple for them to heal it that it would be as though he'd never hurt it at all.

A rickshaw rattled up. Ali took the wallet from Wallace's pocket and paid the driver what he asked. Malaria had swept over Wallace. Ali called to one of the hotel boys to help him take Wallace to the room. It was on the third floor, and twice they had to lay him down on the landing so they could rest.

"Will he die?" the hotel boy asked. He seemed thrilled by the prospect.

"No," said Ali. "Once he was in a coma and he did not die then."

All night Wallace lay shuddering. Ali stripped off the bed-clothes and doused him with water. Wallace's hands and face were brown but his chest was terribly pale and so thin that the bones protruded. Ali put his hand over Wallace's breast and felt the beating wings of the bird trapped inside. The skin was as hot as iron in a fire.

Ali wondered what it might mean if Wallace died. Surely the clerk would not ask him to pay the bill for the hotel. Would Wallace want him to go to England by himself, to take his collections and classify them with Mr. Darwin? It seemed to Ali that Wallace would want that above all other things. Ali saw himself standing next to Wallace's coffin wearing his new suit of clothes.

Not long before dawn, a multitude of birds began singing outside their window, flying away in a cloud to another rooftop and back again. Ali went to the window to pull back the curtain and Wallace sat up.

"I'm thirsty," he said.

The desk clerk sent up water and soup. Strands of noodle stuck in Wallace's beard and Ali pulled them off.

"Today has arrived," said Wallace. "I'm awake to see it."

"England," said Ali. He knew how much the word meant to both of them.

"Home," said Wallace. He swung his legs out of bed. "Will you go home, lad, or will you stay here?"

"I will go home to England," said Ali, smiling.

"Someday, perhaps." Wallace was smiling too. "You might enjoy yourself there. Someday I might come back to fetch you. We'll be old men then."

He slowly pulled himself up and took two steps to the chair where Ali had laid out his clothes. He picked up his trousers and found them still damp from his fever.

Ali sat on the edge of the bed, staring at him.

"I will go with you to England today," he said.

"You would be a great help," said Wallace, "but I suppose I will have to look after myself from now on. I never had a servant at home. It's difficult to picture, isn't it?"

"I will be your servant at home."

"No, I cannot take you with me, lad." Wallace stepped into his trousers. "It is not done."

Ali didn't know what to say. Surely Wallace was joking, but if he wasn't … his village in Borneo, slick with mud. Unloading ships with the other Dyaks. All without Wallace, never again Wallace. His heart beat fast inside his suit of clothes.

"I must not forget to pay you before I go. I have several years owing, haven't I? And a letter! I must write you a letter for your next job. Without your help the obstacles would have been insurmountable. Insurmountable," said Wallace. He was buttoning his shirt. "And for our last breakfast? What about eggs? Do you fancy eggs? Wouldn't take long to cook an egg." He went to the mirror to tie his tie and stumbled a little. He leaned against the dresser, breathing fast.

Ali did not move to help him. He thought of lines of insects crawling over trees, lines of treasure moving through the forest. But it was no longer his place to discover anything new, that part of his mind he would forget about. The things that he knew now he would forget he had ever known.

"England," Wallace said, and stood straight again.

Wallace stood at the rail looking down at Ali, both of them waving, Ali on the dock in his new suit and Wallace in his own from Surabaya. At home he would hang the suit in his wardrobe and only take it out to model as a curiosity from the Orient. Didn't Ali look the little Englishman in his new clothes! But then the Company men in their white hats crowded around Ali and Wallace lost sight of him. The air was thick with moisture and ash; the monsoon was on its way. The crowd surged over Ali so that Wallace could no longer make him out.

A tall man in white linens stood nearby, waving a handkerchief down at the crowd. He grinned at Wallace.

"To whom are we bidding farewell?" he asked.

"Only my boy," said Wallace. "What about you?"

"To no one. But with everyone so gay, I felt I ought to take part."

"My name is Wallace."

"John Sparks."

After a few minutes the steamer moved out into the harbour and a forest of masts blocked their view.

"I have a friend who is in the saloon, I expect," said Sparks. "Shall we join him?"

Sparks' friend Hillyer leaned over and lit Wallace's cigar. On the first puff a sweat broke out over his face, so from then on Wallace just rolled his cigar around the ashtray. Hillyer, meanwhile, smoked several. Like Wallace, he wore black; also like Wallace he looked to have been out in the sun a great deal.

"There are tigers in the interior," said Hillyer. "Lots of tigers. But no one will beat the bush. Beaters can't be had for anything, not like in India."

"You couldn't engage the villagers?" asked Sparks.

"They all work for the Chinaman."

"What of your boy?" Sparks asked Wallace. "What was his asking price?"

"Ten pounds." Wallace held a brandy in his hand and watched carefully as Hillyer sipped his own. "I spoiled him."

"What, each year?" said Sparks. "It would cost me my whole pile to have a gang of them!"

"Ten pounds for seven years."

"Oh, well, that's quite different," said Sparks.

"The same boy for seven years?" said Hillyer.

"It is a specialized field," said Wallace. He fluffed his beard out from his chest. "Once the lad had his training, it seemed a shame to let him go. Most of the time we were out in the jungle and the only other people to be had were stark naked."

"Where was this?" asked Hillyer.

"The Papuans."

"Even the women?" said Sparks.

Wallace shifted in his chair and nodded thoughtfully.

"Were they nice looking?" asked Sparks.

Hillyer smiled.

"No," said Wallace. "Goodness, no! They looked more like men than the men themselves." He waved his hands vaguely over his chest. "And their bodies had no, no support."

Sparks looked mesmerized. "Slack," he said.

"Exactly," said Wallace, and then paused for effect. "I did not envy those men."

Hillyer rocked in his chair and laughed. Wallace smiled and spun his cigar in the ashtray; he had told a fine joke. Sparks grinned down at his glass on the tray.

"It's a shame you didn't get on with your lad," said Hillyer.

"How do you mean?"

"Well, seven years, you either loved or hated one another. He's not on the ship, is he? So I reckon it's the latter one."

"Not at all," said Wallace. "Not at all."

He set his brandy down and stared across the room. Hillyer and Sparks went on talking without him.

Above the door was a painting behind murky glass: a dark hill, with a native village at its foot. Wallace looked at the picture for a long time.

He thought of Ali.

BALINESE

The dirt road was red and dusty, undulating gently with the landscape. Every now and then a stone shrine appeared by the roadside, three or four feet high and tapering to a point, its base decorated with orange and yellow blossoms, sticks of pungent incense and bowls of rice. Insects droned over the offerings and tall palms waved above the road. On either side terraced rice padis clambered one on top of the other as far as the eye could see.

Potgieter went up the road carrying his suitcase in his left hand, his starched shirt riding uncomfortably across his hot shoulders. He hummed a song.

Oh, give me land
Lots of land
Under starry skies above,
Don't fence me in.

On the ship from Holland, musicians in white dinner jackets had played this American song. They'd just come out of the Red Sea into the Gulf of Aden, and at that moment it had seemed a fitting accompaniment for adventure of any variety.

He no longer paid the shrines much attention, he'd seen so many in the eight miles he'd walked so far. They seemed to be increasing in frequency. Certainly that must be a rooftop behind those trees; he had to be nearing the village.

The boat from Holland had taken him only as far as Batavia, on Java. The colonial authorities had been very civilized and had come to his hotel to inquire about his travel plans in the Dutch East Indies. Was Jan Potgieter interested in the colonial service? A plantation? Was he a missionary?

"No, no," he had answered, prompting one man to look up from the form he'd been filling out and the other to set down his drink. "No, you see I am a painter. I have seen some photographs of this place, of Bali. I will go there to paint. I think it must be a lovely place."

"And the women there," the one with the drink had said. "Lord, the women."

In the padi to the left of the road, a line of people suddenly appeared. In unison they stood up and stretched. Potgieter felt his eyebrows rise in surprise, creasing the sweaty skin of his forehead. Young men and women dressed in sarongs and broad hats raised their hands above their heads, some waving tiny scythes with remnants of weeds clinging to them. Their bare torsos were orangey-brown and smudged with dirt, the skin of the breasts taut, the muscles deeply drawn and sinewy. They smiled at one another, chattering, then finally they brought their arms down and started single-file along the stone edge of the terrace. Potgieter realized that he had stopped walking. A shout went up in the padi.

The Balinese came bounding onto the road, spilling all around him, the four or five young men instantly forming a circle, touching his shoulders, smiling, their dark lashes flickering. They were all the same height: ten inches shorter than Potgieter.

He smiled broadly at them, nodding his head from one man to the next and then to the women waiting beneath the coconut palm. He murmured to himself, "I'm not frightened. I have no reason to be frightened. I'm not." Then the men pointed up the road, the way he was going, and Potgieter nodded vaguely. One of the men took his suitcase and another shuffled up the road in a strange dance, hooting like a monkey and kicking up the dust.

"Hanuman," said one of the women. She laced an arm around the bare waist of her companion and the whole party started toward the village.

Potgieter sat at his easel beside the village's north temple. His suitcase had held only canvases, brushes and paint — the largest tins available from Coenraad's Art Supply of Rotterdam — so he'd had no European clothes to change into when his suit became too soiled to wear. When Ketut had collected his filthy clothes for washing, she'd left him a long green sarong to wear instead. But he hadn't known how to tie it properly, folding it down snugly over his hips, so he'd fastened the fabric around himself with his leather belt. She'd laughed so hard that her hands had fluttered in the air like birds.

He lived in a wooden house just outside the stone walls of Ketut's family compound. Ketut was the only fat woman in the village and Potgieter thought it likely, from what little of the island he had seen, that she was the only fat woman on Bali. She had a young daughter called Jata whose breasts were just beginning to grow, a lovely girl, though two of her front teeth were rotten and brown. Often Ketut would set her daughter to work beside the path in front of Potgieter's house, weaving a mat or picking weevils from a basket of rice. Potgieter assumed Ketut didn't ask him to pay rent because she expected him to marry

Jata before long. So as he leapt off his porch each morning, ready to see what was new in the village, who he might meet, what he might paint, what sort of fruit might be for sale in the little market, he would quickly say hello to her.

"Good morning," he'd say in Balinese. It was one of the few phrases he knew.

"Good morning, sir," she'd say. "Do you go to work in the padi?"

"I'm sorry," he'd say in Dutch, "I don't understand what you're saying."

So she would turn her eyes back to her work.

Potgieter sat in a sarong at his easel, painting a picture of Dalem, the young man who had carried his suitcase. The temple's high walls, carved with monkeys and grimacing demons, surrounded a deserted gravel courtyard and a long row of elegant shrines, each spiked with lazily burning sticks of incense set out that morning by women on their way to the fields.

Dalem stood leaning in the arched doorway, his sarong hanging loosely off his hips, his arms folded. With great patience Potgieter was committing every detail — of the wall, the steps, the sarong, Dalem's face, his fingers, his chest, his feet — to the canvas. He tried to suggest a glow emanating from behind Dalem's figure with a pale yellow wash, so thin he brushed it on three times and still wasn't sure if it was visible. Then he decided that the artificial glow was unnecessary, that the most he could do to convey his own wonder was to portray things just as they were. *Why should I try to make it shining and new, when it is so ancient?* The most evocative picture would show exactly what he saw.

He put his brush down and lit a cigarette from the packet in his paint box. Dalem descended from the doorway and took a drag.

"Dalem!" came a voice from around the corner of the temple. Dalem's father, Nyoman, strode toward them, a short, thick man with a thatch of black hair piled high atop his head. Dalem quickly handed the cigarette back to Potgieter.

"Good afternoon," Potgieter called out, in his best Balinese.

Nyoman pretended that Potgieter was not there. He took Dalem by the wrist and started to lead him away.

"What's going on?" said Dalem.

"Your brother is in trouble," said Nyoman.

Dalem had tried to explain to Potgeiter that he had a brother who was crazy and was always pissing on things. Dalem struggled to pull free, but his father was very powerful.

When Potgieter had been in Batavia, his friends from the government had unrolled a map of Bali on their table in the hotel bar. He'd selected the village by averting his eyes and putting his finger down at random on the map. Unfortunately the village was isolated, at the foot of the mountains, many miles inland. No traffic passed through it.

"We'll have trouble keeping tabs on you out there," the one with the forms had said. "Report in once a month for a start, to let us know if you need help."

"If you can come up for air," the one with the drink had said, and he gave a long whistle.

Potgieter had spent his first month in the village; now he would have to return to Denpasar, the capital of the island, to report to the authorities. He had trained in Holland as a cartographer and he wondered whether, if he was not producing paintings of a minimum quality, he might be set to work mapping the more recent of the Dutch acquisitions in the Indies: the Bird's Head Peninsula, Tanimbar, Aceh — names as exotic as Bali itself. But the village was where he wanted to stay, so with determination he rolled his canvases under his arm and started down the road.

He walked for hours on roads heading south, until he was picked up by a buffalo cart outside Ubud. The back of the cart was filled with sculptures of various shapes and sizes, bound for repairs in Batubulan, a town of stone carvers. The driver kept turning around in his seat to point out the beauty of the various pieces, but Potgieter paid no attention. He had never had much of an eye for sculpture.

On the road out of Batubulan, once more on foot, Potgieter heard an automobile approaching from behind and turned to wave it down. By an amazing coincidence, the car contained two Dutch civil servants on their way to Denpasar.

"We're going to the Stadthaus," said the bald one. "Will that be all right?"

"That is the place I want to go," said Potgieter.

"I see," said the one with the pipe, who was driving. "You want to go home."

"Yes, but home to my village. North of Ubud."

"Do you have a plantation? I didn't think a plantation on Bali would be worthwhile," said the driver. "Nobody can grow rice like these Balinese. You can't beat them."

"I'm a painter," said Potgieter.

"Housepainter?" asked the bald one.

At the Stadthaus, Potgieter was sent to a room upstairs where two men and a woman were waiting for him. The woman was there because she was the wife of one of the district officers and considered to be very artistic. Potgieter unrolled his canvases on the long table and the men weighted the corners down with books.

"Don't you like the expressionists?" asked the woman. "It doesn't seem that you do."

"This buffalo has such long eyelashes," said one of the men. "Were they really that long?"

"They were the reason I picked that buffalo," said Potgieter.

"The buffalo is good," said the woman.

"I like this boy," said the second man. It was the painting of Dalem.

"I hope you won't take offence at my asking, but being a fellow artist I'll assume you won't mind," said the woman. "Are you a homosexual, Mr. Potgieter?"

"No," said Potgieter.

"Looking at this picture I'd say you were," she said.

"That's the sort of thing the Japanese wouldn't appreciate," said the first man, tipping his head toward the picture.

"Here we go," said the second.

"What do you mean?" asked Potgieter.

"The Japanese aren't nearly as open to the idea of homo-sexuality as we Dutch."

"What do you mean we're open to it? In the courts it's a felony," said the second man.

"I'd heard just the opposite about the Japanese," said the woman. "I'd heard the officers slept in one another's beds."

"Oh, really?" said the first man. "Well, in the army I suppose it's the same no matter where you're from."

"Why do we discuss Japan?" asked Potgieter.

"You know," said the second man. "Manchuria, Korea, Indo-China ... ."

"They seem to be headed this way," said the woman. "To put it bluntly."

"And they will be here soon?" said Potgieter.

"Oh, maybe never," said the first man, "maybe in a year or two. Still, it's something to think about." He waved a hand blandly at Potgieter and put on his hat.

"I like the paintings," said the second man.

"We'll send them back to Holland for a show," said the first man. "Just leave them here. I have to get to my lunch now."

41

"Yes, I'll have to meet my husband soon," said the woman, looking down at her tiny wristwatch.

"Will you need paints and things, Mr. Potgieter?" asked the second man. "Because the one of that young man really is excellent."

"Listen to you," said the first man.

Dalem was not working in the padi anymore. The women came by to ask if he would pitch in — they were in the middle of harvest and his seasoned hands would be useful — but Dalem said no, for Potgieter needed his help. One of the girls asked if Potgieter wanted to paint her again, but Dalem said no, that Potgieter probably didn't. At last the women went away.

Dalem went back into Potgieter's house, shut the door behind him and quickly undid his sarong. The hair around his privates was fine and downy. He sat in a chair beside the window, pulled his legs slightly apart and tilted his head back, the light falling across him.

"Good," said Potgieter, who sat at his easel in the opposite corner of the room. The edges of the canvas were black and dark brown, with Dalem's figure and the shape of the window painted in brilliant whites and blues and yellows in the centre. The light gleamed across his skin. Potgieter had been tempted to put a pastoral scene in the window, the rice harvest or a buffalo passing, but instead represented it just as a square of light, keeping the viewer's attention on Dalem.

Potgieter recalled how, two days before, he bicycled down to Ubud for supplies. The district officer's wife had arranged for a box to be sent up for him each month from Denpasar. He picked the box up at a house in the center of town, owned by an Englishman, Mr. Ross. He had come to Bali to study gamelan music and he once played for Potgieter, kneeling beside a row of horizontal gongs and striking them with hammers. Ross was always followed around by three or four young women and he often had a flower in his hair.

This time the box contained a letter from Holland, from Potgieter's brother.

"Is it news about their terrible weather or their ugly women?" Ross asked in English. Potgieter was not listening, but he nodded and pursed his lips.

Went to your exhibition yesterday evening, hundreds of people there. Mother couldn't believe it. Bali looks like a nice place. Who is the young man? Everyone was asking me, as though I ought to know. Mother told everyone he was a prince who had commissioned you to paint a series of portraits and that you'd made a fortune. A group of painters say they want to go to Bali now too, to have a look, but at the same time everyone's saying that no one ought to go anywhere until we see what happens with Herr Hitler. Father's eyes are as bad as ever. He made Trixie read him the newspaper from start to finish.

Now, as Dalem sat beside the window, Potgieter imagined this very painting on the wall of the Rijksmuseum in Amsterdam, and his teachers, relatives, friends from the army filing past it, some turning away, some whistling. He was homesick for Holland. He wanted to drink cognac, go to the cinema, hear a jazz band, eat potatoes. But he knew that after a few days there he'd become homesick for Bali instead.

He thought of himself walking up the dusty road, all those months ago now, suitcase in hand, and felt sorry for that Potgieter, so unsure of what the future would hold.

Let me ride through the wide open country that I love,
Don't fence me in.

"What's that?" asked Dalem.

"Song," said Potgieter, dabbing at the palate.

Dalem gave a broad smile. "What song?"

"American song," said Potgieter.

"America," said Dalem. He had never heard of it.

A few months later when Potgieter bicycled to Ubud he discovered that Mr. Ross was not at home. The women sat in the courtyard of his house, scraping out coconuts, and the youngest of these ladies spoke English very well.

"Neville returned to England," she said.

"Why?" asked Potgieter.

"He wanted to be with his family at this important time."

"Was somebody sick?"

"He want to be in the Royal Air Force," said another of the girls, and they all shaped their hands like airplanes and flew them through the air.

Potgieter collected his box and found a letter from the district officer's wife between the paint cans.

When Mr. Pieterszoon and I heard war had been declared, we immediately started packing for home. He resigned his commission here and will try to rejoin his regiment at home. I hope you have not made any German friends, because they will be arrested soon. I am trying to get a few letters off while the other passengers are boarding. Hope to see you at home. We live in Enschede.

Potgieter realized that the box of paint would have to last a long time.

Jata met him on the road back to the village. She looked very pleased, her pink tongue showing through the gap where her front teeth had been.

"Dalem had to go to Padangbai," she said.

"He did? Why?" By this time his Balinese was much better.

"His cousin is there. His father said it was time he learned to fish and to sail a boat."

Potgieter looked across the padis to the east, in the direction of Padangbai.

"When did this happen?" he said.

"His uncle came on a horse this morning and Dalem got on the back."

"But I only left this morning!"

"They took him as soon as you had gone." Jata bit her lip. "Do you like horses?"

Potgieter didn't answer. Every time his left pedal descended it let out a shriek. Jata trotted along beside the bicycle. A breeze was blowing and the dirt on the road looked rich and inviting. Potgieter stopped and put his feet down on the ground.

"Do you want to ride up here?" he said. He tapped the flat of his fingernail against the wide handlebars. Jata climbed up and carefully held her sarong out of the way of the front wheel.

Potgieter's hair had gone very blond after so long in the sun and his arms and torso were as dark as earth. He squatted in the padi, weeding. Small thorny plants grew in the spaces between the rice shoots. He wound the stalk of each weed around his finger and pulled, meticulously, one after the other. The irrigation water was up to his ankles. Half a dozen men and women from the village squatted on either side of him, humming to themselves, their hands working, their arms and faces smeared with dirt. But for his size, his hair, Potgieter looked just as they did.

It had been three years since he first came to the village. He had stopped painting because he had run out of paint and because Dalem had gone. He no longer knew where his European clothes were; he assumed Ketut had them. She had once asked Potgieter if he'd ever been to Batavia, because that was where her husband had said he was going, years before.

Potgieter's hands were so leathery that he couldn't feel the thorns. When he'd first entered the army in Holland he'd sat on his bunk and studied his hands, his poor painter's hands condemned to become soldier's hands. Now such thoughts plagued him endlessly as his hands pulled weeds. His past flickered through his mind's eye, compressing years and people, expanding certain moments to fill an hour. He wished, at times, that he could sit in a cinema and watch these things on a screen; he'd be able then to appreciate then how beautiful that girlfriend had been, how sad and tired the headmaster, and the loveliness of the day when he and his father had had that terrible quarrel. He knew that, aesthetically, his life was one to envy. But he felt only longing.

He told Ketut he was going to ride to Padangbai and soon the whole village knew. As he was tying his clothes into a bundle Nyoman came to the door.

"Mr. Potga," he said, "are you going to Padangbai?"

"Yes, I am," said Potgieter, and because he was in high spirits he smiled at the man. "Do you want to come with me?"

"I know you are going to see Dalem," said Nyoman, bowing to Potgieter. "I ask you, for my family, not to go."

Potgieter got up and went over to the door. He towered over Nyoman.

"I only want to say hello to my friend."

Nyoman kept his head lowered.

"I beg you," he said.

46

Later, Dalem's mother brought Potgieter a chicken clucking in a basket, to take to her son. With the basket tied to his bicycle, he pedalled down the muddy, rutted road. It was the rainy season. Jata would not come out of the compound to say goodbye. Her mother said many evil spirits were about that day and an unmarried woman shouldn't take any chances. "But I am not afraid of them," she said, and shook the rolls of her stomach with her hands.

It took Potgieter a day and a night to reach Padangbai, on the eastern coast. It was a dismal morning when he arrived and only one fishing boat was on the water. The rest were pulled up on the sand, bright blue and yellow, each with the jutting head of a swordfish carved into its bow, the eyes in each head rolled back toward the sea.

When the boat came in, Dalem stepped into the shallows and trotted up to where Potgieter stood leaning on his bicycle. Potgieter tried not to grin, but he couldn't help it.

"What are you doing here?" said Dalem.

"I have come to say hello. I wanted to find out if you liked it here."

"Well, I like the boats. I don't miss the padis, you know. How is my brother? Is he the same?"

"I'm afraid he is."

"I don't miss that."

Two other men pulled the boat onto the sand and walked up to the village, carrying the nets. Potgieter saw them look in their direction, heard them mutter the word *husband*.

Dalem was not looking at Potgieter; he was looking out over the water. Potgieter saw that he was more muscular now, his shoulders broader, but he held himself with familiar grace.

"You know," Dalem said, "the government will pay a lot of money to anyone who sees a military boat. If I'm lucky I'll see a few of them."

"I hope you can let me know, when you see one."

"Maybe," said Dalem.

A small orange crab appeared from behind a rock and made a wide circle around them on its way to the sea.

"Then maybe you can come and carry me away," said Potgieter. "The way they carried you away."

Dalem gave a short laugh, looked him briefly in the face, and Potgieter took hope.

"Maybe you will come back to the village to be painted," he said.

Dalem blew his nose into his hand and threw the mucous onto the sand.

"You know, I have a bad cold. I should not be travelling."

The chicken clucked a few times from inside the basket, trying to sleep with its head under a wing. Dalem's uncle, at least, would be happy to see Potgieter. He had not had chicken in some time.

"I don't have any paints left anyway," Potgieter said.

Padangbai was a grey and filthy place, full of diseased dogs, fishermen with missing fingers, houses falling apart and animal droppings everywhere. But maybe that impression had more to do with the slate-grey sky and the rain. And Dalem.

Jata's cousin Airlan was a stone carver. One day he came to Potgieter's house in his white shirt and black sarong, tapping two chisels against each other — *ting, ting, ting.*

"Hello, Potga," he said. "I wonder if you know about carving."

"I used to know about painting. Now I can't even remember that."

"Come on," said Airlan. "You can help me."

They went around to Airlan's compound behind Ketut's,

through the special gate through which evil spirits could not enter, and knelt down together under a bamboo canopy attached to the main house.

Airlan taught him to shape blocks of stone with a chisel and mallet. Potgieter worked thick calluses into his hands. It was not so different from painting, he thought, taking something shape-less and making something people could recognize as a fragment of their own lives, something that wouldn't have existed at all but for his efforts. They were carving a stone bull to go outside the headman's temple. The muscles in Potgieter's back and arms ached for a long time.

Finally he looked at what he'd carved and realized that this sculpture was a part of the landscape as permanent as a mountain-side, that any stranger could happen upon it. That was what defined Bali: the spirit of the eternal running through everything like a vein of silver.

Unlike any frail piece of canvas in the Rijksmuseum.

Someone from another village said that the Japanese had bombed the city of Surabaya, on Java, and that all the citizens had run into the countryside. The villagers asked Potgieter how big Surabaya was — that is, how many people had run away — and though he had not been there he knew it was a large city, so he pointed out to the rice padi and said that, if all the rice plants as far as you could see were to get up and run, that's what it would be like.

"And they're all as small as that?" asked Jata, beaming.

He had not heard from anyone in Holland for a long time. A Balinese man in Ubud who had worked for the government told him that a peace treaty had been arranged with Germany, but no one knew what that actually meant. Maybe Holland had claimed new territory in Germany. Maybe the armies were fighting in trenches outside Amsterdam, with barbed wire and mustard gas.

Potgieter missed Holland less and less. Whenever he craved veal or beer or potatoes, he would remind himself that in Holland he would have to wear a suit and tie and shoes while consuming them. Then he would look down at his brown feet with pride.

For months Airlan and Potgieter worked on a huge carving of Hanuman the monkey god on one of the inside walls of the north temple. There was a ceremony when it was completed; everyone in the village came to watch the priest chant and sprinkle the new carving with holy water. They sat in the courtyard lit with candles.

"Hanuman has always been my favorite," said Ketut.

"I like Sita," said Jata.

"When you're an old woman, you'll like Hanuman. He's got spark."

"Like you have?" said Jata.

"There's monkey in our family a long way back," said Ketut.

"Please don't say that, Auntie," Airlan said quietly. "There are many people here."

"You like monkeys, don't you, Potga?" asked Jata.

"No," said Potgieter. "Are you a monkey?"

"His teeth aren't big enough," said the headman's wife, pointing to the statue. "I like Hanuman to have great big teeth so he can bite a chunk out of that demon."

"He kicks," said Ketut. "He doesn't bite."

Jata took Potgieter's arm as she sat beside him and leaned her head on his shoulder so that her black hair fell in streams down his white tunic. He took her hand and she pressed her fingernails into his palm.

They were going to be married in a few months' time.

He didn't think about Dalem anymore. He worked with Airlan for long hours, day after day, one sliver of stone chipped away after another, the rock cold and solid under his hand. Sometimes, when he was needed, he'd go into the padis with Jata to plant rice, to weed, to harvest. His rolled-up canvases sat in the rafters of his tiny house.

One day he saw an old man leading a buffalo down a path; three or four chickens rode in his open suitcase tied to the buffalo's back with a rope. There were no handles on the suitcase and it was nearly black, stained with years of chicken droppings. Potgieter laughed to himself, but when he told Jata she said it was a terrible way to treat a suitcase that had come all the way from Holland.

He and Airlan took their cart and went to the same place they always did, a cliff at the foot of the mountains, and brought back a slab of grey rock. Potgieter studied it for a while, contemplating its volume, which parts of the stone were meant to stay and which were meant to go. He started carving a shrine in front of his house for the god that would bless his marriage. After Potgieter had chipped away its shape, Airlan completed the delicate work: a tiny monkey on the top, a line of birds around the middle.

"These birds brought you from Holland," said Airlan.

"I came on a huge boat," said Potgieter, and he spread his arms wide.

"I know that," said Airlan.

The priest came and blessed the shrine. Ketut's family set sticks of incense into the narrow holes Potgieter had carved and people from the village placed fruit and dishes of rice around its base.

"It will be a bountiful marriage," said the priest.

Potgieter bowed low. The wedding ceremony was to be in ten days; the date was one of the most auspicious on the calendar.

"You'll be a pretty husband," said Jata.

He nodded his head gratefully to everyone, but he did not look at Jata.

It was four days later, a hot morning, bright and green, when the Japanese came up the road. Potgieter and Jata and a few others were in the padi some distance from the village, kneeling in the soft mud. His eye caught a spark, a movement, and he lifted his eyes from the rice plants to look. It was sunlight glinting off a bayonet. There were six soldiers on the road marching ahead of a jeep, all gliding silently, almost beautifully, beneath the coconut palms.

"They must be on their way to somewhere else," said Jata. Then she pressed her lips together and Potgieter saw how frightened she was. He knew, had known since leaving Batavia, that the road went only to their village and no farther.

The Japanese went nearer and nearer to the village, the broad leaves of the palms rustling softly over their heads, red dust rising and patiently falling in their wake. The soldiers moved behind the first house and disappeared from sight. Everything was silent. A dog barked, once.

Potgieter stood up, his feet sinking into the padi. The sun was already hot over their heads. He felt nauseous and wiped his hands on his sarong, smearing the fabric with dark mud. He imagined Ketut running from her family compound, waving her arms, saying, "I know where the Dutchman is! I'll take you to him! Come! To the Dutchman!" And the Japanese would follow her. But no, he thought, it wouldn't be her: it would be Nyoman.

Potgieter began to walk across the padi to the village. Jata stood up.

"I'll see what they want," he said.

The others went on working. Jata did not follow him.

He stepped onto the road and a small boy came running from the village, followed by two more boys and a little girl, all wearing triumphant grins. When they reached him the children took his hands and began to drag him forward, his feet shuffling in the dust.

"Japan," said one of the boys.

"Japan," said the second, nodding.

"Japan," said the girl.

"What do they want?" said Potgieter.

"You!" said the girl.

"You, you!" said the third boy.

As they came around the corner of the first house and into the square where the women sold mangoes and onions and bananas, Potgieter saw the whole village gathered around the six Japanese soldiers and their sergeant. The priest and another man were nodding and pointing at the jeep. The headman stood next to the sergeant, gesturing up an alley, in the direction of Potgieter's house. Three of the village dogs were trying to sniff the soldiers' boots and the children were laughing and shrieking, trying to keep the dogs away. Airlan stood behind the jeep with his arms folded. At the back of the crowd stood Ketut, a plump black chicken hanging from either hand. Nyoman was nowhere in sight.

When the rest of the children saw Potgieter they left off chasing the dogs and rushed over to him, grasping at his hand and elbow or moving behind him to push his legs and his behind, push him toward the Japanese, though he walked of his own accord.

The sergeant stepped out of the crowd and the soldiers formed a rank behind him. All of them seemed pale and shaky, and the sergeant, in particular, looked to be on the verge of fainting.

"From Dutch?" said the sergeant, in Dutch.

"Yes," said Potgieter. He had not spoken Dutch in a long time. "But I live in this village." He pointed down at the dusty red ground and two of the children mimicked him, pointing down at the ground as well.

The sergeant took a step forward and seized Potgieter by the wrist, leading him to the jeep, then releasing his arm and motioning for him to climb into the back. Jata appeared between Potgieter and the sergeant, her arms out to fend the sergeant off, but the soldiers knocked her aside. Potgieter stepped up into the jeep. It happened very quickly. Potgieter sat in his sarong with his hands on his knees and Jata lay on the ground, crying through her brown teeth. Ketut stepped up and knocked one of the soldiers across the back of the head with her two chickens so that his helmet came off. The sergeant gave an order and one of the soldiers slid behind the wheel while the sergeant took the other seat.

Potgieter thought what a fine painting this would make, so full of colour and activity, the Balinese all in yellows and reds, the Japanese in their drab uniforms, the dogs and children scrambling around everyone's knees. The morning light glanced off the bayonets and the windshield and played across the faces of the villagers, the soldiers, himself. A few of the women were crying; the men's faces were grim. It was a well-set scene, like Rembrandt's *Night Watch*. A famous painting.

The jeep moved out of the village and the soldiers jogged after it two by two. Everyone was yelling, but Potgieter couldn't comprehend what was said. He saw the crowd close around Jata, and the children and dogs run after the jeep and the soldiers. Then he was past the last house and out of the village, under the palms, moving along the wagon track that had never known an automobile before that day, and the air felt cool and dry.

This is the end of things, then, thought Potgieter. The Japanese had come after all and he was leaving the village behind. And the worst of it: the Japanese had come and Dalem had let them, had given Potgieter no word of warning. Had not spirited him away.

The soldiers trotting behind the jeep stared straight ahead, gripping their rifles with both hands. They looked ill. It occurred to Potgieter that their assignment was simply to travel from one village to another, collecting wayward Dutchmen, because the Dutch are a militaristic people, empire-builders, a threat.

"I'm not Dutch!" shouted Potgieter. "I'm from that village! I'm not Dutch!" He tried to stand, shouting out nonsense, putting his arms out to steady himself. The sergeant took his pistol from its holster, turned, reached up and struck Potgieter across the mouth with the handle of the gun, then the shoulder, then the chest, clubbing him. Potgieter's hands flew up to cover his wounded mouth and he dropped back into his seat. The sergeant gazed at him for a moment and then faced forward again. Potgieter's teeth felt loose, jarred, and a little blood dripped down onto his sarong.

Across the padis to the east he saw a horse cantering steadily along an embankment, then stopping, stepping down onto the next wall, carefully making its way overland to the village. A brown figure sat upright on its back, so intent on the village it saw nothing on the road.

Potgieter stared for a long time at the horse's shimmering flank.

"Do they speak Dutch in this village of yours?" asked Cornelius. He was one of the men who had given Potgieter a ride south to Denpasar so many years before, the one who had smoked a pipe. The Japanese had taken his pipe away, though, so now he always had a twig in the corner of his mouth. Potgieter had recognized him immediately, but Cornelius had not recognized Potgieter, though he did smile when he remembered giving a painter a ride to Denpasar.

"One of them speaks a little," said Potgieter. He turned the letter over and with the last of the ink in Cornelius's fountain pen began to carefully write the name of the village in swirling Balinese script.

"You can write Balinese!" said Cornelius, taking the twig out and placing it in the other corner of his mouth. "That's very impressive. I mean, we were in the service for years, but we, we had so much to do, you know, we couldn't absorb everything at once."

"I can only write this one word," said Potgieter. "But I recognize most others."

"And they can *read* Dutch in your village too?"

"Read it? No, I don't think that anyone can."

"Oh, I see," said Cornelius.

Potgieter unfolded the letter and looked it over again. It was written entirely in Dutch.

Dear Dalem,

I am sorry I missed you at the village. Go to my house if your father does not welcome you. I will be back there soon. I have met some Dutch men and they say the Japanese will not be in the Indies for long, the Dutch will soon drive them out. I am in Sanur now, near Denpasar. I did not realize how many Dutch people were still in Bali. There are 200 or more. They are putting us on a ship. One man told me we are going to Pare-Pare, another told me to Celebes. Perhaps Pare-Pare is on Celebes. I will let you know when I arrive. I miss you very much.

Yours sincerely,
Jan Potgieter

As they waited on the pier at Sanur some women came up from the beach, selling mangoes and handfuls of lichee nut to the Dutchmen, who sat in a long line on the tarred planks. An old man with a hotel in Kuta had loaned Potgieter some money. As one of the women shuffled along the pier, a basket of mangoes balanced on her head, Potgieter smiled up at her — showing the gap where his tooth had been knocked out — and revealed the coins in his palm. She stooped down in front of him. He took a mango, then with his free hand pulled the folded letter from the waist of his sarong and pressed it into her hand with the coins. She slid the letter into her basket, straightened up and moved along the line. The nearest soldier was only a few yards away, his back to them.

The woman did her best; she gave the letter to her sister-in-law, who was headed to the market at Denpasar to sell eight tuna.

"This is Dutch," said the sister-in-law, unfolding the letter and peering at it.

"I know," said the woman.

"I have told you," said the sister-in-law, sighing, "that we don't work for them anymore. Every day I have to tell you that."

"They're good looking, though, some of them," said the woman.

"Where are they going? Celebes? That boat won't make it," said the sister-in-law.

"I've seen better," agreed the woman.

The sister-in-law had not heard of the village, but she was sure that someone at the big market in Denpasar would have. She carried the letter around to a dozen stalls, but everyone just shrugged. Finally a middle-aged man with a faint moustache told her he thought the village was near Ubud, up in the mountains. He was going in that direction in a few weeks' time to pick up his sister and take her to the festival in Gianyar, where their mother had been born. "Why do people have to move around so much?" The man shook his head.

Before Batubulan the letter flew off the seat of the man's cart and stuck on the branch of a tree. His two buffalo were very young — he didn't trust them not to run away while he retrieved it — and there was a ditch below the tree, so he couldn't drive his cart underneath it. He waited for nearly an hour until an old woman came along with a bamboo pole over her shoulder, so long that either end bumped against the ground. He called to her and she held the reins while he hopped down from the cart and pulled the letter free. The woman was too short to have retrieved it herself.

"How long did you wait? A long time?" she asked.

"Not so long," said the man. "Thank you, mother."

"All right, all right," said the old woman, bowing her head a little. "All right, all right."

"What do you think of these Japanese?" said the man.

"They're better than the damn Dutch, aren't they?" She made a fist. "They beat the pants off those Dutch!"

As he rode away, the man considered what a good joke that was, because the Dutch always wore pants, never a sarong, and this only showed they didn't belong on Bali. Then again, the Japanese always wore trousers as well. He wondered if the old woman had thought of that.

In Batubulan the man met a troupe of dancers travelling north to Ubud. They were on foot, pulling in a cart behind them the huge shaggy head of the Barong costume. With its face like a grinning lion and terrible eyes gazing at him, the man had to quickly pass off the letter and be on his way. Afterward he thought that he'd been silly to have been frightened, but his sister told him that the Barong had always given her nightmares and that the idea of its head in the back of a cart was indeed terrifying. The man smiled. He loved his sister.

The dancer who carried the letter didn't recognize the name of the village, but she thought the writing on the front was probably in Dutch. She didn't know any Dutch people in Ubud, but she knew a man from England lived there.

The next afternoon the troupe walked into town, and the dancer went straight to the Englishman's house, through his gate and into the compound. No one was there. She walked through the house and called out, but everyone had gone. She put the letter on the shrine in the courtyard, atop a film of dry and disintegrating blossoms. Someone who knew the village would come along sooner or later, she thought, and send the letter on its way.

She went out the gate and ran to catch up with the others. She was dancing the Legong that night and would have to have her eyebrows plucked.

PAK ARAFIM THE PHARMACIST

Because he was dying, Amin decided to make one last trip into town to see his friend Pak Arafim the pharmacist. In preparation, he rolled seven cigarettes with strips of banana leaf, put on his white sarong and blue jacket in the dark of his house and wrapped a checkered cloth around his head. Such a cloth, his mother had once told him, could fend off the heat or the cold on a long walk, and if it wasn't too hot or too cold then he could use it to wipe his nose. As a child Amin had always had a wet nose, but it had dried out over the years until his head was full of cinders. Nonetheless, ever since he had been in the jungle he had worn a cloth to keep his head safe.

It wasn't long after sunrise. He shut the door and left his house; he took careful steps because he did not wish to jar the pain in his side. When his three chickens came trotting out of the coconut grove, he patted each on its leathery head. They clucked sadly. He had been a good master and hadn't eaten any of them.

The narrow path through the jungle wasn't difficult for him to walk. He knew it well and could prepare himself for the obstacles that lay ahead: the fallen palms, the termite nest, the rotted log where butterflies perched. He could concentrate and step around these things and his side would not burn.

But the unknown beyond the path worried Amin. He had walked into town many times, but now could not remember the way — were there pitfalls ahead? Would trucks still be travelling the road? Had the world gone astray, so that thieves lurked behind every tree?

But he knew that Pak Arafim's pharmacy would be in the same place as always: to the left of the steps to the public market and one block back from the water. Amin loved the town. The water in the harbour was a beautiful crystal blue and the roofs of the houses were all of different colours, brown or red or grey. Some were of new tin from the mainland and others were of very old tin, so old that a boy named Amin had tacked them on in the first place.

Was that possible? Had he worked in the town when he was young? Was he remembering correctly?

It was the middle of the morning. He cradled the pain in his side as sweat ran down his face. Without thinking he put his tongue out to catch the drips. He remembered how, as a child, he had done the same when his nose had run and how his mother had rushed at him and given him such a pinch to make him stop. She had worried that his thoughts would run out of his nose. Amin pulled his tongue in and shut his mouth.

Trails appeared and stretched away from the path and he wondered where they went and whether he ought to take one. He wanted a cigarette, but told himself to wait until he'd reached the road. He stopped to listen. Trucks travelled the road and when Amin was near enough he would hear them. But he heard only a whoop and a cough in the trees above him.

Monkeys, grey and slender, leapt down onto the path,

screeching and climbing back up the trees only to fall down again. The brave ones pulled at his clothes. They opened their mouths and showed their fangs. Had he once played with these monkeys? Was this a game they'd enjoyed?

Why do you hinder me? he asked.

The monkeys ran back and forth among each other, chattering, trying to decide on an answer. See how quickly they moved! Amin was surprised that they'd even noticed him — the growth of trees caused more stir than he did. They crawled out of the bushes and over each other and pointed their fingers at Amin.

We stop you, they seemed to say, because we do not want you to litter this jungle with your corpse!

I can understand that, said Amin. I promise that I will do my best not to die here, but on the road, or in the town.

What will happen to your body there? they shouted.

They will wrap it in the shroud and they will say the *Janazah* over it, I hope, and bury it where it will not be in anyone's way, said Amin. They had buried his father in exactly that way when he had finally washed up on the beach.

Here comes Nenek to decide! said the monkeys.

Oh, Nenek, the grandfather monkey, thought Amin. Again the sweat was pouring down his face. How do I know that? Do I know him?

Nenek was old and very stout and as he ambled up the path the young monkeys placed fruit on the ground around him.

What is your business on the path? Nenek said.

I go to town one last time, said Amin. To visit my friend Pak Arafim the pharmacist. I will die peacefully if I can see him. I am very old.

Then you should not be on the path! shouted the monkeys.

It is one last thing I wish to do, said Amin.

Nenek raised his arms and growled, and the monkeys picked

up their fruit and flew into the trees. Nenek stepped off the path.

No one remembers the days that we used to know, said Nenek. The young have ruined the world.

The sun had gone down and it was nearly dark when Amin reached the road. While he waited for a truck, he squatted in the long grass and took one of the cigarettes from his pocket. He felt for a match, but there was none!

He glared at the cigarette and began to pray that it might burst into flame of its own accord. He prayed for a moment to Allah, then to his mother. He thought hard to picture her and imagine where she might be now. He remembered how she would sit in her chair chewing betel nut and spitting out the window, but with no teeth and a mouth full of pulp she had no aim, so for years her red saliva dripped from the windowsill and down the wall.

He tried now to get her attention, he waved his hands, he showed the cigarette to her, he begged, and finally she turned in the chair and looked at him. Amin squatted by the dark road and licked his lips, ready for the delicious smoke. But his mother said, Amin, are the nets not ready yet? We need them this afternoon!

He put the cigarette in his pocket and found a place in the grass to sleep.

The night was cold and soon he wished that he had never left the coconut trees, or the chickens, or the broiled fish, or the iron spike he used for husking, or his threadbare brown jacket, or the empty bottles of sweet soy sauce, or the little cage he caught mice in, or the path down to the ocean where he washed his clothes and tossed a net out for fish, or the tree where the hornbill sat in his nest without any eggs.

Amin woke up struggling for breath. Had the cinders spread to his lungs? Beside the ocean he had once seen a crystal growing between the rocks, jagged and dull white, criss-crossed with spider webs, and now he pictured it filling his ribcage. He wondered how long he had been alive, then thought of the bandits who hunted innocent people. He listened to the trees moving against one another.

A truck had stopped. The glare of headlights filled the space around him. He had been asleep again. His body still lay in the grass, but his head lay in the road where it could easily have been run over, his body flopping helplessly like a fish. My checkered cloth has saved my life, he thought. Truck drivers saw the cloth on my head and steered around me! But he reached down and found that the cloth had been spread over his body against the cold and that his head was uncovered.

A shadow in heavy boots walked between Amin and the lights, and stopped there for a moment to zip up its trousers. The boots took a half step, then ran forward.

Sir, *pak*, get up sir! My god, you lie there in the road? Come, get up!

The man picked Amin up from the mud and put him in the cab of his truck. He smelled of jasmine or cumin or some spice Amin couldn't quite name. He had lost the names for nearly everything.

First a blanket was pulled over him, then a cup of tepid coffee placed in his hands. The truck lurched forward and Amin knocked his head on the dash. The man's big hand tilted him back onto the seat.

Easy, grandfather. We get there soon. You sick from something?

Amin nodded. The truck seemed to be made of many hundreds of metal parts, jumping up and down together.

You got malaria?

No, no, said Amin.

Dengue fever?

Amin ran his fingers over his left side to show where the pain was, then stabbed his fingers up and down his body to show he had a belly full of cinders, and crystal shards in the lungs.

You got cholera? said the driver.

Pak Arafim, said Amin.

Pak Arafim? The pharmacist? You need to go to town for that, *pak*. There's no Pak Arafim where we're going. But I remember you, I think, you used to live behind the market with your wife, yeah?

Amin's head hung forward on his shoulders, like a vulture. He didn't believe he'd ever had a wife. He didn't know what the driver was talking about.

Pictures of women and decals with Arabic phrases were pasted on the dashboard. Amin couldn't read Arabic, though when he was young his mother told him that the boy who could would be the star of the mosque each Friday and that every girl would fancy the star of the mosque.

I remember when I was a little kid, the driver said, your wife was the prettiest woman around. We all dreamt about her! That really *was* you who lived behind the market, wasn't it?

But Amin was asleep, his cheek against the vibrating metal.

My village! said the driver. He hopped down from his seat to the ground, where brown-and-white dogs circled his legs, yapping and wagging their tails. Amin had not seen dogs for a long time.

It was a clearing in a vast plantation, with much of the open ground filled with pyramids of green coconuts. A family was eating breakfast under a plastic tarpaulin, but when the boys and girls saw the truck they slid down from their seats to run over.

An old man and an old woman each straddled a coconut palm, rags tied around their ankles to help them grip the tree. They shouted hello to the driver as they finished hacking at the fruit with long knives; a coconut shot to the ground with a crash. A teenaged girl rose from the breakfast table and picked it up, chopped it in half with a hatchet and presented it to the woman, maybe her auntie, at the head of the table. The auntie took a long drink.

The driver held hands with a little girl. The children were trying to show the driver whose wooden top could spin the longest, but none performed well on the muddy ground. The old man and woman were shouting and throwing twigs at one another. A baby at the table shook a fish skeleton in its fist.

It seems like a nice place, thought Amin, straightening up in the passenger seat. We must be on the outskirts of town; perhaps I could walk to Pak Arafim's. He checked his pocket for his cigarettes and reached up to tighten his head cloth. But he was not wearing it. The driver's pink blanket was spread over him. His cloth had been left beside the road! He took a deep breath so that tears would not come, but the breath was too deep. The back of his lung started to rip. He grasped for the door handle.

The old couple lowered themselves to the ground and threw their knives into a tree stump. Oh, those youngsters, thought Amin, as he smiled at the two old people, see how nimble they are! And I was like that myself only a year ago, climbing the trees, swimming out with the nets. Too long without seeing Pak Arafim, that's the trouble. But I am nearly there.

The old couple came to the driver with open arms. *Anak, selamat pagi*, good morning, son, they said. They paid no attention to Amin. The old man had a wispy beard and his wife was nearly bald.

Pagi, pagi, said the driver.

Success? said the old woman. Are you celebrating?

The driver undid a padlock at the rear of the truck and threw open the big doors. Amin steadied himself against the side of the cab, but he pulled his hand away when the roar started, as thousands of coconuts clattered against each other and poured out onto the ground.

The children pushed each other out of the way to see who would sit atop the pile. The old man put his arms around the driver.

This will teach those bastards a lesson, the old man said. Coconuts come from the south of the island and always will! Look at the quality! They're terrible!

The old woman took one and pounded it against a rock until it burst into pieces. The meat inside was white and succulent.

They're all rotten, she said. You couldn't feed them to cattle.

Not to a rat, said the old man. What do they sell for at the market? Five hundred?

Two hundred, said the driver. They have the government subsidy because they are new. Government will support new business. You remember when the man from the party came around in the truck?

We have been selling to the port for fifty years! said the old man.

I've told you, it's the gangs, said the driver. They tell the government and the government says we are already a success, we don't deserve their money.

Amin looked around the clearing. The girl and her auntie were clearing dishes from the table under the tarpaulin. Two shacks made of tin stood behind them. Farther into the trees was a broken old house, tree trunks fallen across its roof. Chicken bones and rusted buckets lay half sunk in the mud. The driver yelled at the children to hurry up, pile the new coconuts next to the old. One dog lay down to lick its sores and the rest began snarling at it.

Is this all you could get? the old woman shouted. Are you lazy?

This was all they had going to market! said the driver. You know they hit me in the stomach before I got away!

Why don't you cry if you think that will help us!

As Amin watched the girl and her auntie disappear into a shack he remembered a woman and child of his own. It was dusk in the memory, the orange light filtered through the drizzle, and they were clearing plates and taking them into his house in the coconut grove, and his daughter, what was she doing? She was bending over, he remembered, giving a bit of rice to the cat, its tail crooked in three places. And Amin, what was he doing? He was fixing something, his hands covered in grease, what was he fixing, a truck? A motorcycle! The motorcycle was their only way in from the jungle — he had to fit everything from town in a box on the back and she was wasting grains of rice! He ran across to where she was petting the cat on its scabby head and he knocked his daughter to the ground. She lay there and looked at him, a black handprint on her face. He took a step toward the cat and it ran away.

He tried to remember his wife. She always clapped her hands when it was just the two of them. He remembered how the light came in the window.

The driver took Amin by the elbow and led him to the old couple, who nodded respectfully. The few strands of the old woman's hair fell over her forehead.

Ma'af, grandfather, sorry, said the driver to Amin. I should have made introductions. Here are my parents.

It's the coconuts, said the old man sheepishly, pointing toward the pile. We get so excited! It is an honour.

But you were sleeping in the road? said the old woman.

Ibu! said the old man. He furrowed his brow and she scowled back at him.

Amin watched the old couple. Their splayed feet sank together into the mud; they understood one another.

The driver raised his hand, only a few inches, and the others cocked their heads to listen. They heard an engine approach. The children ran to the sheds. The driver gently steered his parents behind the truck. They watched over the hood as he came back to rescue Amin, but by then the sound had died away. The old woman burst into tears.

If anyone in town asked Amin about coconuts, he was to say that he hadn't seen any on the whole island. The children were covering the truck with palm leaves. Oh, the auntie was beautiful, rapping the children's hands with a switch! If Amin had had a daughter she might be the auntie's age now.

I have to lie low, said the driver. They're looking for me. Those men in town are gangsters. I'm sorry to have driven you away from town, it's just the way you were lying in the road there ...

Amin turned on the bench and leaned his back against the table. He'd had a nap before the meal and was thinking of having another.

The old woman grudgingly poured more tea into his glass.

One of the dogs sauntered up, its tail swaying.

You'll never make it to town, it said to Amin. If you want to stay with us, you can lie under the table and sleep.

I, I have to see my friend Pak Arafim in town, said Amin. He had not seen a dog in many years and was somewhat flustered.

Pak Arafim? Oh-ho! Yes, you're the one they're talking about!

The dog started yapping to the others, who lay flopped under the trees. This is the one they are always talking about! And the other dogs joined in the laughing.

Who talked about me? said Amin.

Our cousins, said the dog, who live in the forest.

How do they know me? said Amin.

Um, maybe you will be on your way? asked the driver. His parents sat next to him with their mouths open. The old woman nudged her husband with her knee — this Pak Amin looked more and more like the man who had run the market in town, who had started up the gangs, who had burned down their old plantation, who had been against independence for Indonesia and sided with the Dutch because they gave him money. Look at the way he held his fingertips together, no one else did that! And speaking with the dog as though it could speak back! Well, perhaps that was because he was old. But surely it was the same man! What if anyone was to see him at their table? It was a bad omen. Allah would frown on their son for rescuing such a villain.

The old man studied Amin and nodded his agreement.

Amin fumbled to set down his glass of tea as the driver helped him to his feet.

I was going to have a short nap.

There are plenty of places to sleep along the road, said the driver.

The dog lay under the table, panting smugly.

Amin walked with the driver until they were some distance from the table. Being guided by the driver's strong hands around his arm, he felt hollow-boned and weightless, as though the driver could pick him up and set him down wherever he pleased. But when the younger man let go and Amin had to continue walking on his own, he felt as though his hollow bones were on the verge of crumbling, as though they were made of dried-up leaves.

Somehow, by a miracle, *insya Allah*, they had kept him upright all these years. But perhaps in a few minutes they would turn to dust beneath him, and leave his jaw hanging broken from his head.

He managed to stagger across the clearing toward the road. The children sat silently beneath the trees, the midday heat humming through the palm leaves.

Here the dirt of the road was chalky and grey and the trees alongside it were coated with dust and looked to be dying. A single kingfisher, bright blue, flitted between the boughs. It was far from any water and probably in trouble.

Amin placed one foot a few inches in front of the other, stirring tiny storms of dust, and thought about crawling into the cool undergrowth. If he was lucky, he would be dead before he had grown too thirsty. He stopped and gazed at the forest, where the shadows were so pleasant and dark. The hot dust settled on his feet.

But he kept moving along the road because he had set out to reach the town and to see his friend Pak Arafim. He did not want to die and be remembered as an old man who hadn't taken his plans seriously enough to see them through.

From somewhere the idea of his wife and daughter came to him again, and was there a son as well? He remembered a son wearing a red shirt, standing by a pile of new boards. Were the three of them remembering him now, unkindly? Where would his wife be? She would be as old as the woman at the plantation, the driver's mother.

And could the chickens beside his house be thinking of him? Did they remember him as a terrible master too?

He walked with his head in his hands.

He tried to think only of those things that he knew for certain — his desire to see Pak Arafim and his desire to smoke one of the cigarettes. He should have asked the driver for a match! He decided to combine the desire for a cigarette with the desire to see Pak Arafim, who would surely have matches, *Made As Sweden* brand, the only matches they had used when the two of them were boys. They would sit and smoke while the Chinese woman taught them Mah Jong and one of her girls would bring in strong coffee.

When he reached town he would go to the pharmacy and ring the chime as though he were any other customer. His friend would be so surprised. Amin would embrace Pak Arafim in such a way that he would know Amin was not well and give him a little pill for the pain. Then they would light their cigarettes with their *Made As Sweden* matches and play mah-jong until it was morning.

He tried to take longer strides. He breathed deeply through his nose, always careful not to rip the tissue of his lungs, which he knew to be delicate. Soon his head felt better and he let his arms swing as he walked, taking mighty steps. He looked about him and tried to guess how far he had travelled from the plantation. It was already the middle of the night.

The sky was clear and the moon stood in a perfect half at the end of the road, as though waiting for its other half to arrive by truck. Amin was enjoying himself now and listened to the jungle as he moved past it, all its roars and snores and whistles. His own feet made no sound as he walked and he thought that he might have become a ghost, intangible and wise. He enjoyed the idea. Inside the jungle, he knew, men and women had lived, grown vegetables, kept chickens and goats, knelt beside the trees and peered into the undergrowth and one day died, and as he walked he watched for them, hacking through the nighttime forest with their knives, descending ghostly paths to flag a ride.

To walk at night was cool and peaceful, but already Amin had tired. Only the idea of his destination urged him on, for if he were to die by the roadside, to rot unattended and end up a ghost, then he would have no destination, only endless wandering. He knew why the ghosts had to travel at night and did not rest in the earth as other spirits did — they had not received the *Janazah* or been properly buried.

He shuffled faster along the road now, for he was a mortal man who wished only to rest someday in the cradle of the ground.

He felt an insect on his bare calf and brushed it away. When he still felt its touch he looked down to see it was the whiskers of a yellow dog against his leg. It gazed up at him happily. As Amin slowed his pace, other dogs trotted ahead until they surrounded him, four or five dogs in each direction, so he felt as though he were standing knee-deep in water, only it was dogs.

Aren't you a calm one, said the yellow dog.

Another dog sniffed at Amin's hand and gave the thumb a thoughtful lick, then nodded to the others in mild approval. Amin pulled his hands to his chest.

Why shouldn't I be calm? he asked.

Are you not a Muslim? asked the yellow dog. Do you not believe that Satan lives inside us?

And in pigs! said another dog.

Do you not believe that Satan lives inside pigs and dogs? asked the yellow dog.

I, I do not eat pigs or dogs, said Amin.

Oh, good! sneered a dog, as it sniffed Amin's ankle. I was frightened!

When I was a child, I did not consort with pigs or dogs, my mother said that the devil looked out of their eyes, but —

Is that not exactly what I said? said the yellow dog.

But I, I looked very carefully, without going too near them, and never saw anything the matter.

You're coming with us all the same, said the ankle-sniffing dog. You're the one we've been looking for. Grandfather's grand-father was looking for you.

They walked along together, a caravan padding slowly through the dust. Amin thought about it for a moment and remembered why it was so strange to see the dogs in the first place.

He had not been kind to dogs, as a younger man, though he had not seen the devil in their eyes. But he *had* seen that they were dirty and full of parasites, infested on the inside with worms and on the outside with ticks and more worms, and that they chewed at their scabs all day and any hair left on them was crusted with pus. He'd started a campaign — yes he, Pak Amin, who'd run the town market — to drive the dogs from town. He remembered this. He'd said they had to be taken from the market because they spread worms to the meat that was for sale and when the town had agreed he'd demanded the dogs be taken out to the forest where they would have to look after themselves. But in truth he'd paid the streetsweepers to club the dogs on the head and dump them in the harbour. Most nights he and Pak Arafim would leave their mah-jong to watch the bodies floating beneath the pier.

It would never be a modern town or part of the civilized world so long as disease ran rampant. Steamships from Europe stopped at the town then to take on fuel and water, it was a well-known depot for coal, and all of the rich people in the town agreed with him. The livelihoods of their children depended on it. His wife told him that, even though she was a good Muslim and had no love of dogs, everyone at the mosque was saying that slaughtering animals that were not hurting anyone and could not be eaten was barbaric. He told her that nothing barbaric had happened in the town yet, but when a nervous dog came down the steps into the market he smashed its head with a board and told his wife that now something had.

All this came into Amin's head like a draught of cold water. He knew that if only he still had the cloth on his head he would not have to be remembering any of it.

The dogs stopped and sniffed the air cautiously. Farther ahead there were trucks parked on the road and campfires in the jungle.

It's a trap! said the ankle-sniffer. This old thing is bait!

Are we not hungry? said the yellow dog. Should we not perform the execution before we proceed farther?

Right, said the ankle-sniffer.

Kindly step into the woods with us, said the yellow dog.

Soon Amin was stumbling through the creepers and wet undergrowth as the pack loped behind him. When they were well away from the road the yellow dog ordered Amin to his knees.

Are we going to do it here? said a three-legged dog. I thought we were going to walk him to the lair.

Do you not think that the men are waiting there to rescue him? asked the yellow dog.

Tear him to pieces and then let's get out of here, said the ankle-sniffer.

And carry the meat with us? said the three-legged dog.

Why don't we gorge ourselves, said the yellow dog, and regurgitate at the lair? Do we not have the pups to think of?

That's what I've been trying to say, said the three-legged dog.

Amin rested on his knees. He didn't mind walking but standing in one spot was too much of a strain, so he was happy to kneel. He looked up at the night sky through the trees and saw flitting birds and graceful flying foxes.

The yellow dog threw himself onto Amin's neck and the two of them toppled over, and as the ankle-sniffer drove his teeth into his shoulder Amin thought that if only he were wearing his checkered head cloth he might be perfectly safe. The awful teeth took a strong grip on the shoulder and then wrenched back so that pieces of his jacket were pulled away along with whatever meat was there. The rest of the dogs were trying to get their snouts into his underside, but he pulled into a tight ball and tried to roll away from them into the wet leaves. The dogs made noises like saws cutting timber. The yellow dog pushed him onto his back and nearly had its teeth around his throat when it suddenly toppled over into the brush beside Amin. There was a large purple hole in the dog's side.

Then the ankle-sniffer was shot in the chest from another direction and the rest of the pack ran except for the three-legged dog, which took Amin by the ear and tried to drag him away, but its teeth ripped through Amin's ear and the meal had to be left behind.

Amin lay in silence, the sky empty of night birds or flying foxes. He lay like a wasp crushed underfoot and left for dead, his useless stinger twitching in the air.

Men ran up with rifles and looked at the bodies of the dead dogs.

They're a good size, said one of the men, pulling the yellow dog by the tail.

We might get more than the usual, said the other.

An old man came and stood over Amin. Amin recognized him as one of the town streetsweepers from years before. The riflemen picked up the dogs as though they were enormously heavy.

You get same as always, said the older man, and he peered down at Amin.

Lying in the back of a truck, at night, Amin found the town difficult to recognize. The lights went by at strange angles. The truck slowed at each corner as it steered through crowds of people. Boys with moustaches, wearing caps, held their cigarettes and looked over the side at Amin. A Chinese man with a baby on his shoulders screwed up his face at Amin and tried to make the baby smile. Laughing girls in makeup looked down at him before the truck pulled away.

He could not see the buildings from where he lay, only the peaks of roofs and sometimes a street sign: *Jalan Perdagangan, Jalan Teuku Umar*. He recognized the post office, but now the sign said HOTEL. He passed tamarind trees, their dry boughs lit up by lights from the restaurants. A breeze from the harbour moved over Amin and he reached up with his good arm to touch his ear. Dried blood flaked off under his fingers and fell onto the blanket.

The whine of motorcycles went by. The truck lurched forward, then stopped.

Apotik disini, pak! one of the riflemen shouted back to him.

A pharmacy! Amin tried to sit up, but he put too much weight on his shoulder and fell down again, hitting his head on the tailgate.

Oh, pak, said one of the men, and he gently put down the tailgate with one hand while he held Amin's head steady with the other. Amin carefully swung his body around and lowered his feet to the ground. He walked a few steps on the cold pavement, shivering and holding his shoulder. The truck's engine roared and the rifleman closed the tailgate and started for the cab, but then he came back, took a blanket from the back and threw it over Amin's shoulders. It had been lying on one of the dogs.

The truck sped away. Amin stood hunched over, under the sickly streetlamps, looking down at his thin legs. His white sarong was black now and ripped in several places. His feet were badly scraped and he had lost a toenail. The scab on his ear opened and a fat drop of blood splashed between his feet.

He tried to straighten up to see where he was.

He was on a block of the old two-storey shop-houses that he remembered so well, but most of the shops were closed, either for the evening or forever, with metal bars rolled over the doors. In the middle of the block, though, a few doors from where he stood, the rollers were up and a fluorescent light flickered over plastic chairs. Three mothers sat there with their babies. He shuffled forward and peered at the sign over the door.

APOTIK ARAFIM, it said.

But his friend's pharmacy was not where he thought it would be. It was not on a corner, not near the market steps, not near the water. The mothers read magazines while their snotty-nosed babies gazed up at Amin. He held the blanket close to his shoulder, but blood had soaked through it and out onto his hand.

He moved toward the high white counter at the back of the shop. A stocky man in a white shirt and spectacles stood up from a stool.

Ibu Wojowasito, the pharmacist called out.

Amin stared up at him. This man was not Pak Arafim.

Ibu Wojowasito came to the counter for her prescription and her baby reached out and grasped Amin's blanket in its fist.

Ahhh! said Amin. His voice was ragged and frightening.

The baby let go.

Sir, please take a seat, said the pharmacist. I'll be with you in a moment.

Ibu Wojowasito gazed disapprovingly at Amin. The baby coughed. Amin turned and moved toward the plastic chairs. The other mothers pulled their babies close. He turned again to face the counter. Ibu Wojowasito had her money out and when she saw Amin facing her again she hurriedly pushed it across to the pharmacist.

Is Pak Arafim here? said Amin.

Take a seat, sir, said the pharmacist.

Amin shuffled a few steps farther and with great care lowered himself onto a chair. A table sat between the mothers and him, and he gazed blankly at it, at the magazines stacked there, the box of *Made As Sweden* matches, the child's rattle.

He looked at the box for a long time. Then he slowly took his good hand from his shoulder and let it slide into his jacket pocket. Several cigarettes were still there. Carefully he took one between his fingers, drew it out of the pocket and placed it between his dry lips. He decided to rest a moment before lighting it.

The mothers watched him while pretending to look elsewhere. Ibu Wojowasito finished her business and went out. A movement on the ceiling, small and green, caught Amin's eye. A tiny *cecak* lizard scurried above him and Amin held his head at a painful angle to watch it. His cigarette pointed at the ceiling.

No smoking in here, said the lizard.

Amin carefully took the cigarette from his lips.

I had not lit it.

No smoking, said the lizard. And may I ask what your injury is?

Dogs, said Amin.

Please don't joke with me, sir. There are no longer any dogs on the island.

Look at my shoulder if you don't believe me, Amin muttered.

May I? said the lizard.

Amin set the cigarette next to the box of matches and nervously pulled the blanket down. Some of the flesh was scabbed over, but where it was not the blood ran freely down his arm. Bone was visible deep in the wound.

The lizard moved along the ceiling to a better angle. It defecated a small white pellet that fell onto the magazines. One of the mothers got up and left.

And is this shoulder your only complaint? asked the lizard. What about those cinders in your head? Do they no longer trouble you?

There's my ear as well, said Amin.

You'll have to see the pharmacist. He'll give you antibiotic, disinfectant and probably a tetanus shot. I've been studying him. Were they rabid, these dogs of yours?

Amin tried to remember the dogs. They'd seemed very calm. No, he said.

The last of the mothers went out with her prescription and the pharmacist sat down in the chair beside Amin. He took Amin's head in his hands. With his finger and thumb he pulled Amin's eyelids apart and looked into his eye.

You're in shock, sir, said the pharmacist.

Where is Pak Arafim? said Amin.

The pharmacist let go of Amin's head and turned him to get a look at the shoulder. Pak Arafim? he said. He was my grandfather. He's been dead for ten years, but I still see many of his old customers.

He stood up and inspected the ear.

Don't you remember me? said Amin.

No, sir, I don't, said the pharmacist. He tilted Amin's head to one side.

Pak Arafim— said Amin, but his voice broke, tears welled in his eyes and a line of snot dribbled out his nose and onto his upper lip.

Don't worry, old friend, said the pharmacist. I know my grandfather didn't always fret about money, so I don't fret about it either. *Insya Allah,* I'll get by anyway.

He wet a swab with disinfectant and began to clean the ear.

Lots of injuries these days, he went on. That truck driver who was so badly burned, he died this afternoon they tell me. Did you know him? A big man. Like this.

He held his arms out at his sides, indicating a shape like a mango.

I don't know anybody! Amin croaked.

And those coconut farmers who were shot down at the south end? Surely you heard about that. Stealing coconuts, that's the official word.

The pharmacist looked out at the street to see that no one was around. You would think, he whispered to Amin, that they could have invented a more credible story than that! Couldn't they have stolen goats, or fishing hooks, or anything else? They had all the coconuts they needed!

The pharmacist waited for Amin to laugh along with him. When he didn't, he remembered that the poor old man was in shock, that it was time he cleaned and stitched the shoulder. He hurried over to his counter for some mercurochrome and some more iodine and a needle and thread. He kept talking so that the old man would not pass out.

This is quite a government, though, isn't it? No country's perfect, but the world must wonder how we got this way, don't you think? Surely in Grandfather's time it wasn't like this, was it? How does this corruption start? What's your opinion?

The pharmacist sat down again. The old man had a banana-leaf cigarette in his mouth and was trying to light a match.

Let me get that, said the pharmacist.

He struck the match and held it out for the old man, who inhaled feebly. There was no draw on the flame but the cigarette seemed to light of its own volition.

A *cecak* ran across the ceiling and disappeared outside. The old man puffed as best he could and leaned back in the chair.

The pharmacist took up his position at the shoulder. He

poured a little iodine directly onto the wound and waited for the old man to cry out.

I have a pain, said the old man.

Well, that doesn't surprise me, said the pharmacist. This arm's been—

No, the pain is here, said the old man, the burning cigarette at the corner of his mouth. He stabbed with his fingers up and down his left side to show where it hurt. I come to see Pak Arafim for this pain.

What is the matter? said the pharmacist.

Give me some of the green pills that Pak Arafim used to have. I've come all this way to get a few more.

What green pills? What did they do? I have many pills that are green, said the pharmacist.

I haven't had them for a long time, since I ... since I moved out to the jungle. I had to leave town and Pak Arafim nearly did too. I had a bad stomach then and he gave me some pills. After I'd taken them all, my wife said I should get more, but it was too dangerous. Too many people were looking for me.

What did you leave town for? asked the pharmacist. He had one eye shut as he threaded the needle.

I can't remember, said the old man. He took the butt of banana leaf and threw it on the floor, then dug in his pocket for another cigarette. The pharmacist stopped what he was doing to light it.

It had to do with ships, said the old man. There were many ships in the harbour then. Are there still a lot of ships?

Not so many, said the pharmacist. He drove the needle through the edge of the skin but drew no reaction from the old man.

We were importing something. But what was it?

Narcotics? said the pharmacist good-naturedly. Slaves? He raised his eyebrows behind his spectacles.

No, it was weapons! All sorts of rifles. Grenades, too, crates of them. I remember unloading them there, by the ... by the customs office. And every few weeks we got our money. It was just Pak Arafim and I. We organized it all.

Where did the money come from?

Oh, from the Dutch. Of course it came from the Dutch. Our government was running things by then, but the Dutch were still up in the hills. Hoo-hoo! There were hundreds of them. Then there was that fight at Gapang beach and one hundred of our boys got killed, maybe two hundred — it was the grenades that got most of them. They were wonderful!

The old man flourished his cigarette in the air. He really seemed to be enjoying himself.

Amin looked out at the sea. The benches in the back of the truck were narrow and with the bandages for his shoulder wrapped across his chest he had to twist himself uncomfortably, but he wanted to see the water. He thought of how he and his mother had gone out in the little boat to bring in the nets when his father was plowing their rocky field. The water would splash over Amin and his mother would say that people who live on islands all come up from the sea.

The water in the harbour was brown now and plastic bags floated in it. He thought of the excitement there had been when the streets were dug up and a pipe was put in to take the waste far out into the ocean. He had persuaded everyone that it would be a good idea, a step forward for their modern town. But the contractor only took the pipe out as far as the pier and then went back to Medan. That was after the Dutch had gone, when the people in town were beginning to talk about what he'd done, he and Pak Arafim.

In the end he and Arafim had decided that one of them would stay in town and live a good life and that the other would accept the blame and hide in the jungle. But Arafim was to have told him when it was safe to come back.

Morning, *pak*, said a young man as he stepped up into the truck. He took a seat on the bench opposite, took a drink from his bottle of soda and gazed at Amin. Do you want to lie down, *pak*? I'm sure there will be space on the bench.

No, said Amin. His teeth were chattering. I want to look at the ocean.

A family with their shopping in tattered baskets pushed past Amin and the young man to sit behind the cab. Another family and an old woman waited on the sidewalk.

Are you from one of the villages, *pak*? asked the young man.

My house, yes. By the sea.

The old woman pushed in next to Amin, her white hair tied on top of her head. She looked at him closely.

Do you go fishing or hunting, or what do you do? said the young man. You have a big family? I'm sorry, but I'm fascinated by the people who live in the forest. I'm at the college in Medan now and I want to write a paper.

There's only me. My family went away, said Amin.

The old woman looked down at her feet, then at Amin again.

Always to the town, said the young man. People can't stay away from towns.

One of the boys fell off the bench and landed up to his elbows in a basket of fish. The father picked him up and sat him on his lap. The mother smiled and wiped her son's greasy hands on her sarong, clicking her tongue in mock annoyance.

Amin felt the tears well in his eyes again and the familiar coursing of his nose. He wiped at his face with his ruined blue sleeve.

You aren't well, *pak*, really you should lie down. Look, there's space for you, there, if you could just — thank you. Now just lie down, *pak*. You sleep a little. It's all right, nobody minds.

Amin lay down on his side, his good shoulder against the bench, the top of his head next to the old woman. His nose was blocked, so he had to breath through his mouth, and his cheek pressed uncomfortably against the wood.

Pak, you need a pillow for your head now. Doesn't someone have some clothes or a bundle of something for his head? No? Here, we'll try this then. This might do.

The young man took his empty soda bottle and placed it under Amin's head. The plastic crunched against Amin's good ear but his neck was more comfortable.

The truck began to move and the bottle rolled slightly, so his head bumped against the woman's hip with every turn. It was not an uncomfortable motion, though. He was able to fall asleep.

Get your feet and legs back! said a deep voice, and everyone began to shuffle around the truck. Amin brought up his head to see what was happening and the old woman placed her hand on his cheek to calm him. A man in a collared shirt was loading a block of ice into the back, on its way to villages on the other side of the island. The ice filled the space between the benches and stood a foot off the deck. When the salesman had gone to sit in the cab the passengers rested their sandaled feet against it.

Amin slept as they went out of town. When he opened his eyes he saw the ocean going by through the slats in the side of the truck, just a sliver of blue between the boards, and palm trees flickering past between the road and water.

The world seemed very simple. He couldn't feel the pain in his side. He hadn't had any pills, but the pain was gone. And he had made it to town. It didn't seem important whether he made it back.

The truck went up a hill, away from the water, and onto the

road through the jungle. When it took a sharp curve Amin slid from the bench and onto the block of ice. The other passengers struggled and rolled him back onto the bench. They pounded against the cab for the truck to stop.

He was dead.

The children sat calmly with their parents.

The salesman pulled down the tailgate and looked at his ice with disgust. The dead man's legs were on it and a line of blood had stained one side.

Well, who's going to buy that now? Who's going to want that? he shouted.

The old woman picked up Amin's head and put it in her lap. She stroked his poor face. She was sure it was him. It had to be him.

MANY MANY ELEPHANTS

Mr. Tong had all the people's passports in a plastic bag, hanging off his handlebar. He's crazy on his motorcycle, he thinks it can go anywhere, between anything, so he went between two cars and the plastic bag got stuck on one of the mirrors. Car went out of Chiang Mai with the passports, Mr. Tong went into Chiang Mai with nobody's passport. He saw right away he didn't have them so he turned around to find them, going back and forth through the cars coming the other direction and of course he crashed, I could have told him that. He ripped up the skin on one leg and lost one of his flip-flops.

"Put them in a backpack," I tell him. "Put the people's passports in a backpack, not in that plastic bag." But because he was a monk for so many years nothing bad can happen to Mr. Tong, no. Now he is lying there without a flip-flop, hoping the army does not find out. Some of the people, from Australia, from Germany, they think the Thai army will never come to their country, that there is nothing to be afraid of. But I was once in the army, and when you are all alone walking down the street and the Thai army stops you and asks you questions, you should look out.

I am at the hotel telling the people what the trip will be like, funny stories so they will think about something else, because when someone else has their passports they get nervous. They get up from the chairs and look out the door to see if Mr. Tong is coming. I tell them how wonderful the jungle is, how I hunt all the animals in the jungle. And I show my knife.

"I hunt bats," I tell them.

"How do you hunt bats with a knife?" they ask.

"Maybe a gun is better," I say.

But I tell them that a knife is better for cutting branches, making medicine. My mother had a belly full of worms, like a ball in her stomach, moving around, but so many it was like a stone. You could see her belly stick out like this. So I got the right branches and bark and boiled up a tea for her. She was lying on the ground with her blanket, and she told me, "My son, this tea is very very delicious, but it is for curing mothers who cannot make milk. You want me to have worms for my breasts too." Then she fell asleep, and I picked her up by myself, because my brother had gone to Bangkok, and I carried her all the way to the hospital, though my mother told me many many times she was never to be taken to a hospital, because the government is a very bad government, but please forget I say that. Shhh, shhh. They are a good government. But they pay the doctors only when the people die. They do not want there to be too many of the Thai people, like in China. You know about China?

These people nod their heads, they know about China. Some of them smoke their cigarettes and watch TV. There is special Thai boxing on TV, from the big stadium in Bangkok. People from England especially like to see this on TV.

One Australia lady, she says, "They can only have one baby in China."

I tell them yes, but then the baby can live one hundred or two hundred years and the China government does not mind. But here in Thailand the government pays the doctors so that the Thai people die when we are very young. If you are rich, you send money to the government before you go to the hospital, so the doctors will not kill you but make you well. I had no money for the government because I was out of the army then. In our village I was a very rich man, but I only had some pigs and cows. People said that soon I would bring a TV to the village. My mother said that she would never stay in the hospital and I should spend the money on a TV. So I went in a truck to get one.

"Did you watch boxing on your telly?" says one of the people from England. He enjoys the Thai boxing very much. He asks me if we can go see the boxing in Chiang Mai.

"I am very very busy now," I say. "Before our trip I must say goodbye to my wife and baby. After the trip Mr. Tong and I take everybody to see the boxing."

"Where is Mr. Tong?" says one of the ladies.

I say what Mr. Tong said: he must make photocopies of passports for insurance purposes.

"He's been gone a long time," says one of the people. "We want to hit some bars."

"See some bar girls," says another.

"There are not so many bar girls in Chiang Mai," I say. "The government says Americans come to our city only for bar girls, like in Bangkok, and our city should not be that way, we want to … we want to have *culture* in Chiang Mai. Now the bar girls, you see them ride scooters and ask you to get on the back with them."

The one from England says, "I heard the ones who ride scooters are really men."

I tell him that that is not true.

One lady, she says, "What about your mother? Was she all right?"

I tell them that my cousin said petrol was too expensive, so we couldn't run his generator anymore. And I tell them that the worms in my mother grew much bigger, you could see them moving under her skin. This meant that something did not want me to bring the TV to our village. I wrapped the TV in a blanket and lay it there beside my mother. One of the elders said I should not wake the TV because at night the Karen people in the hills will hear it and come down to kill everybody — they think we are a Burmese village. The Karen people have been fighting so long they don't know where they are.

In the end my mother told me to leave her at the hospital. After I carried her there, she woke up and she knew she would die. The worms were moving under her skin and now under her legs, fighting under there, but my mother patted her belly and went shhh, shhh, and the worms went very quiet. She said I should go back to the village and watch my TV because she was so proud of me.

"Deh, let's get some beer, all right?" says one of the people. "I can handle waiting if we have beer."

"Will we see elephants on the trip, Deh?" they ask.

I say, "Yes, many many elephants. You ride elephants when we arrive at Elephant Camp."

Then I tell them that my mother was from the Lisu people, and that my father paid fifty thousand baht for her because she was a very fast worker in the field and more important because she was very very beautiful. Some girls, they are not so beautiful, they are lazy, and their husband pays only one or two thousand for them. My father loved to lie beside my mother and they had two sons very quick. But the soldiers from Cambodia, they are in the north of Thailand because they hide there with the USA They all want to fight in Cambodia but Communists in Cambodia are very strong, so they hide in Thailand. One of my father's pigs got

away and they said in the village it was a tiger, so my father went
to look for the tiger and the soldiers from Cambodia shot him up
on the hill. And my brother said they took our pig too, it was not
the tiger.

"You'd think the fuckin' Yanks could buy them a pig," says one
of the men, a very big man.

The ones who watch TV say, "It's pretty convenient to blame
the States for everything."

I tell them that I went home from that hospital and I watched
TV because my mother wanted me to. My cousin and all the
elders came into my house to watch, and it was boxing from
Bangkok on TV! Everyone yelled and was very happy. There was
one match between a short man and a skinny man, and the skinny
man was the champion. In the next match, no one could
believe it — there was my brother! He had cut off his hair and
he looked very good, very good at boxing. He had to fight another
skinny man, and my brother ran at the skinny man, and the skinny
man jumped up and kicked my brother right here, right here, in
the chest.

"Sternum," says one of the people.

"Yes. Right here," I say. "And my brother died."

"Come on," they say. "He died? One kick and then dead?"

So I stand up and say, "I will kick you then and you will be
dead!"

"Deh, Deh," says the hotel woman, "Deh, sit down. Do not
fight with the people."

It is because of the hotel woman that Mr. Tong is the guide
for the trips and I am the porter. The people give more tips to the
guide and the guide can wear expensive shirts. My wife says I
need to have better shirts to make it big in Chiang Mai.

The elders all went out of my house and my cousin said the
petrol was not so expensive anymore, but it was not a good idea

to watch TV because something evil was coming out of it. So I took the TV and lay it down beside the jungle, so it could watch my family die if that was what it liked so much.

"You mean you wanted the Karen to watch your TV?" says one of the ladies.

"No," I say, "not the Karen. Another something that is in the jungle."

"You mean a spirit?" she says. "A ghost?"

"Something like the devil," I say.

"Aren't you Buddhist?" they say. "You have no devil. Christians and Muslims have a devil."

"I know the devil," I say.

One of them watching TV, he wears a very good shirt that says Chicago Bulls, he says, "They tell their kids if they don't eat up their fried dog, some Vietnam MIA will carry them away, that's true isn't it, Deh? That's their religion."

Another says, "No, they tell them they won't get any opium."

"And that makes the kids *cry*," says the Chicago Bulls.

"Listen," says the man, the big one, "why don't we go out and see if we can find Mr. Tong? I could do with a walk. I feel the need to have my passport."

I jump up and I say, "I will find Mr. Tong."

Then I hurry out the door so the big man will not follow. I know about the plastic bag. I told Mr. Tong not to use it and I have a bad feeling now. I run through the chickens on the corner, turn on Tha Phae Road, the way Mr. Tong always goes. Many many tourists on the road. They look for the girls on scooters, but it is too early, it is still in the afternoon. Before I knew Mr. Tong, when I had no work, my wife wanted to be a girl like that to make money. I said, "We have a baby coming, no." My wife said, "I know a baby is coming."

My cousin bought my pigs and cows so I could go to Chiang

Mai, go to Chiang Mai and never go back to the village. They must all be eaten up now, my pigs and cows, and maybe some people in the village ate the pig or cow only so they could have their opium after. You can starve to death, very easy, if someone does not make you eat. You lie there and dream.

There are many shops on Tha Phae Road selling shoes, selling watches. Then I see Mr. Tong pushing his motorcycle up the road, near the Nawarat Bridge, by the post office. Girls in their uniforms all stand at the bus stop and watch him, his leg covered in blood, his one foot with no flip-flop walking in the broken glass beside the road.

I say, "The passports?"

He shakes his head.

I take the motorcycle and push it. We are going back to the hotel but the big man who wants his passport is there, so we do not hurry.

Mr. Tong says, "I should have never left the monastery. They didn't let us ride motorcycles or have people's passports there. We stayed out of trouble."

I say, "But a woman couldn't touch you. Your own mother couldn't touch you."

He says, "It wasn't touching my mother that made me get out of there."

There was no work when I got to Chiang Mai. I stayed at the back of someone's house, under a sheet of plastic, and when I met my wife I took her there to live, but my wife said it was not safe. She said, "We must have doors that lock and walls to stay behind. You do not live in a Lisu village now." She had hair cut short so it went behind her ears, and little white earrings. She was so beautiful I had to say to her, "Soon, soon, we have locks and doors."

After a while I missed my village and I wanted some opium.

Mr. Tong lived in the neighbourhood, he sold opium to everyone so he was easy to find. We sat in his house and smoked many many pipes. His opium was not as good as in our village, but it was still opium. I lay on the floor in his house and had the same dream I always have: going north on the train, going home to my village when I am finished in the army, passing by temples full of monkeys and many many people living beside the tracks. The train is full of monks in orange and old nuns with bald heads. And then, coming home in real life to the village, and every time afterward, in the dream, when I sleep, when I have opium, this man with eyes like a cat, very dirty, creeps up the aisle toward me, and I am not in uniform anymore, but I have my knife and my boots. I could stand up and fight him but I do not. I don't know why. He sits on the floor with the nuns in white, then he sees me and creeps up the aisle. His watching me is the worst of it. Maybe it is him that has been watching for many many years, from the jungle, everywhere I go.

Maybe I would not smoke opium anymore if I could never see him again, but after so many times he is like an old friend, this man from the jungle with a strange face. He has hair on his face, not like a Thai, but from some other place.

Mr. Tong says, "Does the hotel woman ask about me?"

I say, "Not yet."

I say, "Can the trip go?"

He says, "Not without passports. No more trips for you and me."

I say, "Can you help me find work?"

Mr. Tong was hired by the hotel to run tourists on trips around the Mae Tang River, between Pai and Fang, near to the Lisu tribe, where my village is. He wanted me to help him, to be the porter. I said to the hotel woman, "No, I will be the guide, it is my jungle, my home. I will hunt deer with my knife." She said,

"Mr. Tong is the guide. He has expensive shirts, and what do you have?"

So I am the porter, and after many many trips I have a room for my wife and baby, right in Chiang Mai. If my cousin comes, I will show him what I have. The baby is a son, a boy, and he is tough like me already. You see the muscles in his arms when he walks behind his belly.

Before we go to the hotel Mr. Tong wants to stop for a drink. He tied newspaper around his foot but now it has come off. We have Beer Chang and sit beside a fan.

"What will we do?" says Mr. Tong. "The people will stay at the hotel until we are found. They will call their governments. The army will come after us."

I say, "The army is nothing to be afraid of."

Mr. Tong says, "You were in Bangkok on Black Monday! You were with the soldiers that killed the student! They burnt him with kerosene!"

"No," I say. "Shhh. That was not Black Monday. That was later. That was Thursday. I don't remember it."

"I do not want that to happen to me," Mr. Tong says. "We will say someone stole the passports from me. I was on the motorcycle, I was near the photocopy office, and someone snatched the bag from my hand. Someone in a black car. I will tell them that for a long time I was a monk."

I say, "We will lose our jobs anyway. What will you do, Mr. Tong? What can you do for a job?"

He says he can work in an electronics store. He says, "Deh, what will you do? Will you go back to your Lisu village?"

I say, "No. My wife will not leave Chiang Mai. She even wants to go down to Bangkok."

He says, "No. Terrible terrible violence in Bangkok," and Mr. Tong holds up his hand for another Beer Chang.

Just then the people from the hotel, all the men and ladies from England and Germany and Australia, go past the bar and look in. Mr. Tong waves his hand. But we are at the back of the bar and they do not see us. The one man is very very big, but if he decides to come for me I have a knife for him.

They go away up the street. Mr. Tong gets his beer and drinks it all and then puts the bottle down and clutches his belly. He says he has to use the toilet. I try to remember what the passports looked like, what colour they were. Some of them were blue and some of them purple. We could make new ones if we had paper.

My wife will be home now. I will take her back to my village, my wife and son. My house will still be there next to the jungle.

Mr. Tong comes back from the toilet, holding his belly, rubbing it, and he says he is scared now that the army will find him and stick him with knives. Then he says he is scared because he heard of a secret army in Burma, an army of Buddhists who hate all other Buddhists. His friend went to their camp, they were growing beards and instead of a Buddha in their temple they had a picture of Christ. They said Christ would return to Earth and lead them with guns against Thai Buddhists, Karen Buddhists, everyone. He says he doesn't want to make any more trips. He says, "Everyone knows I am a Thai Buddhist," and he holds his belly.

I say, "You are stupid, Mr. Tong. There is no army like that and there are no men like that." But I think of the man on the train.

We go out on the street. It is nearly dark now and I push the motorcycle. Mr. Tong walks beside me, slowly.

He says, "We will go to our houses, not to the hotel."

I say, "We leave the hotel forever."

Mr. Tong smiles.

I stop when there are chickens in the road and I see the man from our trip, the one from England, and he runs at Mr. Tong, shouting. Mr. Tong holds his belly and shows his hurt leg. The one from England asks where the passports are. Mr. Tong shrugs his shoulders and the man punches Mr. Tong so he falls in the broken glass. Girls on scooters are all around us and a woman *hiss-hisses* the chickens back into the shed. The street is very busy with people looking down at Mr. Tong. I put down the motorcycle beside the road and the one from England comes at me. He jumps back and forth. He has seen the boxing on TV and thinks he is ready.

I take out my knife and I reach for the one from England. He tries to get away, he says, "Take it easy, mate! Easy!"

KINGDOM OF MONKEYS

Hal said he liked the clove cigarettes because they smelled terrific, so I said, "Why don't you get somebody else to smoke them then and you can just sit beside them, get some eight-year-old in here to help you out." It was first thing in the morning, we were in a coffee shop in Kota Kinabalu having some foamy tea and the image of an eight-year-old, some Asian kid in shorts and a Bon Jovi T-shirt, it got me laughing. I was the only woman in there, so all the guys in the restaurant turned around to stare. Hal looked down at his plate of hot noodles — that was the only food they had — and the men all sat turned in their chairs, all these Muslim guys, smoke hanging off their cigarettes, thinking, "Christ, no wonder we don't let women in here."

That afternoon we got off the bus and stood beside the river on a couple of planks set over the mud, waiting for the boat to come. Hal lit up again.

I said to him, "What's with you and those things?"

He said, "I'm trying to feel at home."

I said, "Why don't you try speaking the language?"

Hal had not made any effort to fit in except to smoke their cigarettes, whereas I had it all written down on a piece of paper in my pocket: *satu* one, *dua* two, *tiga* three, *empat* four, *lima* five, *ma'af* sorry, *tandas* toilet, *terima kasih banyak pak* thank you very much sir.

"I just want to see an orangutan," said Hal.

Black muck was collecting under my bra and our packs were so heavy we were sinking in the mud. Finally a long boat came swinging up the river and a couple of German models in string bikinis and hiking boots hopped out — Germans are beautiful or ugly, there's no in-between. They murmured *"Danke"* while the guys from the boat carried their bags over the mud. None of them looked at me or Hal, and who can blame them? Hal's no German model.

They were typical Borneo guys, short and stocky with stylish black bowl cuts, but they looked happier than most. They were singing to themselves. The guy steering the outboard told us his name was Sudirman. We sat down with our feet in about an inch of water and the guys piled in and cast off, in a hurry to get back to camp.

"No doubt for some leisurely masturbation," I whispered to Hal and he smiled. All the boys were looking ahead up the river, so I made a motion with my hand and then Hal looked worried because they had turned around again and were scowling at us. Sudirman had a big knife strapped to his shorts.

On the river the critters came and went in clouds. First there were big white birds, then monkeys, then bugs. The guys laughed and waved them away, but the bugs really went after Hal. He's got a good nose, nice and long and Roman, but it was covered with bites and red lines from his scratching and in one place it had started to bleed.

Then a kid at the front of the boat pointed and everybody

followed his finger, something poking up out of the river, disappearing just as fast. I looked at Hal and he shrugged, a Kleenex over his nose.

"Crocodile," said Sudirman. I looked back at the spot on the water and Sudirman started singing, "Ohhhh, ohhhh, crocodile."

The hut they gave us at the camp was about a foot off the ground, which was good defence against rats, Hal said, but then it was just a roof, a floor and mosquito netting. The guys in the camp could see everything, so there would be no naked time for me and Hal, either of the rolling-around or just sitting-there variety.

"Bet it didn't slow those German girls down," I said and Hal went quiet because he was thinking about string bikinis.

We unpacked, got settled in, read our Lonely Planet books. When some hornbills flew by Hal got out his camera and I helped him organize the lenses. A nice vacation, like we'd talked about.

At dinner we met Uncle Ibrahim, the owner of the camp. The bottom plate of his dentures was too big and was always sliding out of one side of his mouth or the other. He complained about the chainsaws in the area and how there weren't any more Borneo rhinoceros. He said the camp was going to close down and it was a sign of the times that the only two losers staying there were Hal and me.

"Me and my boys," said Uncle Ibrahim, "have to find jobs someplace else."

The dinner was hot cabbage and fried fish and Hal was really putting it away while the boys all stood under a lantern watching us. When he stopped to take a bone out of his mouth he said, "What sort of jobs will you get?"

Uncle Ibrahim looked unhappy and said, "Maybe in a hotel. Maybe crime."

Hal nodded and went on eating while Sudirman slid his knife around to the back of his belt so it would be less obvious.

Christ, it was noisy in that place at night, all hoots and hollers and scratching noises under the hut and things dragging themselves around on the damn roof.

"It's a sloth," Hal kept saying. "A three-toed sloth."

I kept telling him, "That's in South America." It was too hot to cuddle up so I couldn't get to sleep, and Hal ought to be thankful because I found some insect that was headed for his brain and crushed its head between my thumb and forefinger.

I looked out around sun-up and all the guys were on their knees in the middle of the camp, bending up and down, jumping, bowing, kneeling again, all the while muttering in one of their languages. Muslims in action.

They gave us taro root pancakes for breakfast. Uncle Ibrahim came running over, all excited about the crocodile we'd seen from the boat. He'd just heard about it and said it was a bad omen. I realized his English was pretty good, because it seemed to me if you were sitting down to learn English the word omen wouldn't be the first one they'd give you. When Uncle Ibrahim wasn't looking, Hal slid a piece of pancake back and forth out of his mouth. It was a pretty good imitation. Uncle Ibrahim wanted us to know why the crocodile didn't have a tongue, he wanted us to guess.

Hal said, "The danger of biting it would outweigh its advantages."

I said, "The crocodile is older than the evolutionary development of tongues."

We both figured we were right, so there were some pretty dirty looks going back and forth.

"That may be," said Uncle Ibrahim, "but in Borneo we know a different reason."

Just then the kid arrived with a new jug of tea. He spilled half of it on my bare leg and I yelled "Fuck!" and jumped up out of my seat. He ran off and I started after him, but he hid behind some other guy and after that I couldn't be bothered.

Uncle Ibrahim pretended nothing had happened and hurried on with his story. He said that in the long-ago kingdom of monkeys, the crocodile was an adorable rascal who eventually had his tongue cut out because he was always swearing his head off.

"To let a curse escape your mouth is not proper in any society. The people could stand it no longer," said Uncle Ibrahim, then he got up and left.

Hal gave me his evil raised-eyebrow look and said, "You better watch your mouth."

What the heck did they think the place was, anyway? The height of civilization? It was no Roman circus.

But to show Uncle Ibrahim I'd taken his fable to heart, I got out my piece of paper and went to find him so that I could say, "Thank you, sir!" *"Terima kasih banyak, pak!"* He was walking up the planks from the outhouse. He didn't have his trousers up yet when I said, *"Terima kasih banyak, pak!"* and Jesus, did he look mad. He pointed a finger at me and held it still.

Hal was sitting on the cookhouse steps with the boys, passing out his clove cigarettes like a Girl Guide leader giving out badges. I went up to try a little one two three *satu dua tiga* on them, show the boys I was one of the gang, but when I walked up they all started laughing and clapping. They pushed Hal to his feet, saying, "Go, go, Hal!"

Hal put on the serious face he makes when he plays charades and shuffled up beside me. *"Saya cinta padamu,"* he said, fluttering his lashes. The boys whooped and clapped their hands. I didn't have a clue what he was doing so I kept my hands on my hips. *"Saya gila! Saya gila!"* said Hal and then he did a weird dance, waggling his finger in a circle beside his head to show he was a lunatic.

I guess that was the end, because the boys all leapt to their feet and mobbed Hal, slapping his back and shaking hands.

Sudirman grinned at me. "He say, 'I love you,' then he say, 'I crazy, I crazy!'"

Crazy to fall for *that* girl. The same stuff with Hal starting all over again.

I waded into them while he was grinning at me as if to say, "No hard feelings, right?" But I shoved him in the chest and he fell on his butt. Everybody backed away.

I said, "Assholes."

I went to our hut, which was not the greatest hiding place. The monkeys got louder. Hal came into the hut and I asked him if he wanted to play some cards, but he said no. He started hunting through his pack to find the bird books he'd paid forty dollars each for. I told him it was too hot to go out in the middle of the day, but he didn't care, he wanted to look at birds. So he took off and I fanned myself with one of his nature magazines, and why he'd brought it all the way to Borneo I have no idea, because it was all about bison. My karate magazines were way at the bottom of the pack.

Uncle Ibrahim came over and stood on the steps. He kept glancing at the panties sitting on top of my pack — they had cartoon cats on them and, to his credit, he was probably worried about their impracticality.

"I am sorry, Miss, maybe it is because they are Muslims, maybe because they are men, but all my boys are yelling in the kitchen." He slid the grey-coloured denture out of his mouth and let it hang there for a second. "They do not want to be chased by you. They do not want to be pushed down by you. They do not want you to watch them in the *tandas*. They do not want to listen to you curse. Think of the crocodile," he said. He took a parting glance at the panties and stomped off.

I looked out across the camp and saw all the boys looking out the window holes of the cookhouse, staring in my direction. One of them said "Fuck " clear as a bell. I jumped down the steps and picked up a rock. Their faces disappeared. It sailed through the cookhouse window, where it banged into pots and pans, from the sound of it, and broke something glass.

I walked down one of the trails to the lake and sat down on a bench. A scene from a brochure. There was a cardboard sign by the bench with plastic wrap stapled around it: ACROSS A LIKE A WILD ELEPHANT LIVES. ESCAPED CAPTIVITY. LIVE ALONE THERE.

That night there were freshwater prawns for dinner and Sudirman sat slicing the skins off them with his knife. Before he'd make a chop he'd hold the knife and look over at me. Then he'd thump down into the prawn. It made Hal nervous. His nostrils got wide and I had to keep smiling at old Hal to keep him in the game. The other boys stood back, out of the light.

The next morning, as promised, was Orangutan Day. Uncle Ibrahim and Sudirman and some of the boys led us out into the jungle, stopping all the time with a finger to their lips, looking up into the treetops through the vines. Orangutans build nests, Hal had told me. They find a nice fork in a tree and pull all the branches in, a nice cocoon, and dream red-haired dreams for sixteen hours.

"Did the German women see any?" I asked Uncle Ibrahim.

He looked confused, shaking his head, patting his shirt pockets, until Hal offered him a clove cigarette and the old guy's face lit up like a pinball machine. Then he was pointing at imaginary orangutans all around us and making jokes. Hal and Sudirman laughed. I wasn't sure where we were. A cloud of mosquitoes isn't much of a landmark.

We came into a muddy clearing with two or three big trees in the middle. Sudirman was in the lead and had stopped to look up. We were all quiet as church organs, studying this damn tree, which more than likely had a bird in it and had never in its life had so much attention.

"Are they dangerous?" I said to Hal. His mouth hung open and of course I wanted to see a butterfly or something fly into it.

"No," he said, "but it won't want to see us."

"Shh!" said Sudirman. Then he pointed up into the tree and if you followed his finger there was a tuft of copperish hair, just to the left, one, two, three branches from the top.

"*Satu, dua, tiga,*" I said.

Uncle Ibrahim said, "Shut up." I pretended not to hear.

"A big one," said Sudirman.

Hal took some pictures of the tuft of hair, grimacing at me because he knew they wouldn't turn out.

The path went on between the tall trees. I was at the back of the line while we tiptoed like idiots through the twigs — we didn't want to wake the orangutan or he'd drop like a cannonball onto our heads. I batted some bugs away from my eyes. Then there was a crashing above us, branches breaking, the tree trunk started to shake, one boy grabbed the other by the arm and they all ran for it like loonie-toons. The thing was coming down the tree, crashing through the branches and I couldn't get my goddamn feet to move. Hal was long gone. Finally my shoes lifted up and I was down the path and around the roots of a mangrove, past more trees and finally beside a ditch where the others stood waiting, all panicked in case the orangutan was chasing me. I stopped next to Hal and looked back, but there was nothing, just leaves whirling beside the path.

We all stood panting, breath shaking out of us, the boys, Uncle Ibrahim, Sudirman all smiling at each other in relief. I glared at Hal, who was smiling too, his nose running.

"Fuck, Hal," I said, my breath coming back. "Where the hell were you?"

Of course everybody went quiet. Uncle Ibrahim looked at Sudirman. The boys looked at me. They knew what was coming.

"Miss, you should remember about crocodile," Sudirman said. He unsheathed his knife and threw his hand around the back of my head. He was pretty quick. Then he brought the knife up to my face.

A bird squawked in a tree.

I pushed the arm of his knife hand out of the way and with my other hand I punched him across the bridge of the nose. Then I pulled the knife hand across to the other side and brought my foot down into the side of his knee.

You should have seen his face. I'd only done that kick barefoot before — a guy comes at you with a knife, when was that? Green belt? Blue? Anyway, with a boot on you do more damage. He went down all foetal, holding his knee.

Hal finally moved, to pick up the knife and give it to Uncle Ibrahim.

Uncle Ibrahim said, *"Terima kasih."*

When we got back to camp there were more pancakes. I told Hal he ought to try to get some pictures in case the orangutan was still around, but he shook his head. He told Uncle Ibrahim he wanted to settle the bill, we were leaving. The old guy was pretty relieved. The Barbarians had entered Rome and done some good-natured ransacking, but now they'd decided to be on their way and asked what it was they owed.

The boys sat on the ground around the cookhouse with their soccer ball, waiting for us to clear out. Sudirman limped around them, trying to get a game started.

On the ride back up the river, the breeze meant the bugs weren't so bad. Hal still sat there itching, so I pulled him over and gave his nose a kiss. I ran my tongue along it, then I started to kiss his mouth but he pulled away, as if there were birds on the river he needed to see. We sat on opposite sides of the boat.

Eventually he said, "They were just trying to get you to shut up."

"What?"

"It's a cultural difference," he said. "That man may not recover."

"He was walking around!"

"I mean his pride." Hal wiped the droplets of water from his face. "A man has his pride."

After a few days we got back to Kota Kinabalu, where it was a bit cooler, and we checked into the same crappy hotel. When Hal came to bed I wanted to show him with a little loving that I wasn't mad about any of it, it was all behind me, but he wouldn't go for it. He said he felt like there were bugs crawling all over him and, granted, there probably were. But that's not what a girl wants to hear.

DISTANCE

"**W**hat do you mean you won't cash my traveller's cheque? What is this? I'm a fucking movie star!" said Timothy. "Did you know your town sucks? Because it does. Prague *sucks*."

"Sir," said the man in the Plexiglas booth. "Passport. Or some ID."

"My passport's in my trailer," said Timothy, patting the pockets of his suit. "Look, this is American Express! I might as well have fucking cash in my hand! Look at my signature at the top. All you gotta do is watch me sign the bottom and I gotta tell ya, that should be all the ID you oughta need. All right? Watch me sign."

"No, sir," said the man, waving a long finger. "That will make your cheque void. Get your passport and come back here. Close at six, open tomorrow at seven-thirty. The next person please."

Timothy stuffed the traveller's cheque into the basin where the Plexiglas met the metal counter, but the little man blocked it with his hand, tearing one corner.

"Oh, now it's fucked!" said Timothy, pushing back his long bangs. "Terrance, this thing is fucked now!"

Terrance shuffled forward in his red trenchcoat, smoothing down his moustache with his finger.

"I've got cash, Timothy. I'll buy you a nice Budvar, all right? Come on, out the door." He put his arm around Timothy and steered him as the people in line stood and stared.

A bell tinkled as they went out the door.

It was a gorgeous afternoon. Traffic whizzed by the shop windows — Volkswagens, Saabs, Trabants — shards of sunlight bouncing off their windshields and glancing off the sides of ornate, centuries-old buildings. Pedestrians filled the narrow sidewalks. Terrance and Timothy came out from under the shadow of the American Express awning to stand in the sunlight next to a sausage vendor. Terrance reached for the buttons of Timothy's jacket.

"Leave my buttons alone!" said Timothy.

"I don't want you to overheat," said Terrance. "We should try to head back to the set. It's nearly one-thirty."

"Fuck the set." Timothy reached in his shirt pocket for his sunglasses. "Did you see that in there? That guy had never seen me before, ever. Does Paramount have zero distribution over here or what? Fuck going back, what good is it gonna do me?"

"The more you work, the more people are going to know you. It's basic."

"No wonder we came here to shoot the fuckin' movie, Terrance. I mean, what year's the script set in?"

"In 1390."

"Yeah, well, it's 1993 and they're cashing traveller's cheques like it was the Middle Ages. What's this guy selling here? What are you selling, hot dogs?"

"*Parek v rohliku,*" said the sausage vendor.

"Well, what I want is a hot dog. Aw, I still don't have a fuckin' cent! Prague sucks!"

"Here's twenty crowns. You buy yourself that hot dog."

Terrance handed Timothy the coins and lit a cigarette. Timothy dropped the coins into the vendor's hand; the hand was missing its pinky finger. The vendor threw the coins into a box, untied and retied his apron, faced the traffic to turn some sausages in a pan and after a minute handed Timothy a piece of cardboard with two pieces of rye bread, a puddle of grey mustard and a long orange sausage resting on it.

"Oh, what is this?" said Timothy. "Terrance, tell me what this is."

"Hot dog," said the vendor.

"It's time to get back to the set is what it is," said Terrance.

They started down the crowded sidewalk, moving in the direction of the Charles Bridge. Timothy balanced the sausage on a slice of mustard-soaked bread and ferried it toward his mouth, his elbows catching passersby in the shoulder.

"Prague fucking sucks," he muttered.

"I think maybe you hate it because you've got that secret," said Terrance.

"I knew you would say that. I knew it," said Timothy, his mouth filled with chewed bread. "Just shut up."

"Klapka is probably a good Czech name. I don't know why you don't want to use it. We live in a global village after all."

"So what?" said Timothy.

"So people don't have to anglicize their names anymore."

"I don't care if it's *anglicized* or not, I just don't want a stupid name and Klapka is a stupid name. Carson is not a stupid name. I mean, John Wayne, he didn't change his name because *Marion* wasn't *anglicized*, he changed it because it was stupid."

"Did you change it to Carson?"

"No, my grandfather did. Long time ago."

"He probably changed it because it's Jewish. People didn't

want to be Jewish back then," said Terrance, throwing his cigarette down behind a woman in a leather coat. "I'm Jewish, you know. Nothing to be ashamed of."

"Jesus," said Timothy, "you'd never think Europe would be so hot, would you?"

"I don't think we can ever understand what Jews have gone through the way Europeans do. I just don't think we can."

They rounded a corner and passed a Dixieland jazz band. A tall elderly man in tinted sunglasses, jean jacket and bowler hat was swaying in front of several horn players, singing a gravelly "Chattanooga Choo Choo" through a megaphone. A plump woman plucked a banjo. As Timothy passed them, the singer lowered his tinted glasses and winked at him. Several Japanese tourists with cameras around their necks stood watching the band and clapping their hands to the beat.

"You could at least go by Klapka while you're here," said Terrance. "Maybe it'll grow on you."

They came into a square where a hundred tourists stood staring up at a medieval clock tower and the blue sky.

"Well, for all I know it means asshole. What's with these people? Find me a garbage for this cardboard thing. Man." Timothy bumped his way through the crowd, Terrance behind him. "Hey, what scene are we doing when we get back?"

"You tell the queen to go jump in the lake, you don't want to rule."

"I said I wanted that scene fixed. Why would he suddenly say 'ain't'? 'Ain't fit to rule.' Guy forgot what movie he was writing."

"Unless you're using bad grammar to underline your point," said Terrance.

They stopped in a narrow alley off the corner of the square, where a dolly loaded with kegs of beer was being backed out of one restaurant and into another. They waited while the beer man in his leather cap closed his eyes and flexed his neck to haul the dolly up the step. Timothy ground the toe of his shoe into the space between two cobblestones. Once the kegs had disappeared through the door, the beer man leaned out again and gave them a jovial salute. He was missing his pinky finger.

"Cigarette," said Timothy.

They were at an intersection, waiting to cross the street to the Charles Bridge. From where they stood they could see the swans in the river and the spindles and crosses of the castle, high above the city on the opposite shore.

"Sorry, Timothy. I'm out."

"Give me some money, will ya? I'll pick some up at that place by the barracks. I can't stand not having any cash on me!"

Terrance fished in his pocket and pulled out a one hundred-crown note, but a breeze plucked it from his hand and lifted it above their heads.

"Oh," said Terrance.

"Wow," said Timothy.

The note fluttered down. Terrance took a step forward to seize it and a white BMW caught him above the knees. For an instant Timothy's and Terrance's eyes met. In another instant Timothy saw the driver, a woman, her hair pulled back, mouth hanging open, nails digging into the steering wheel, and then Terrance pitched into the air and came down on the opposite sidewalk. The BMW careened around a corner and was gone.

The people waiting at the intersection got out of their cars and a one hundred-crown note spiraled down into Timothy's open hand.

"It's funny you should have to come in this afternoon, Mr. Carson. There aren't many other officers who speak English and you know I was supposed to have this afternoon off, but my dentist got sick. So it's purely by chance I'm here to take your testimony."

"I've been having good luck all day," said Timothy.

They sat in the police station just below the castle, high enough on the hill that, looking out Captain Mejzlik's window, Timothy could see the countless angled rooftops stretching far across the city and cathedral towers sprouting like flowers from a lawn.

"How do you like Praha?" asked Captain Mejzlik, his feet on the desk. He fingered the yellow tassel of the sword on the wall beside him.

"It's fine," said Timothy. A series of air bubbles rose in the water cooler in the corner, making a sound like moving bowels. Timothy shifted in his chair. "It's okay. I have another two weeks of shooting. But I don't know how long that'll take now."

"Mr. Singer was an actor as well?"

"He was my assistant. He organized everything I did, everything. I mean, I don't even know what day it is today."

"They can get you another assistant."

"I guess. But Jesus, that's not exactly the point, you know?"

"Certainly," said Captain Mejzlik, twisting the tassel around his finger. "You are from San Francisco? I hear you have a wonderful Chinatown."

"No, I'm from Los Angeles. That's south of San Francisco." He sighed. "Where are you from?"

"Oh, I'm from Zelivskeho," said Captain Mejzlik. He gestured toward the window. "Over there. An old neighbourhood. We all know each other."

"Sounds great," said Timothy. "Look, my concern here, really, is to nab this lady who hit him. That's my concern."

"Of course it is," said Captain Mejzlik, pulling his feet down and taking a file from his top drawer. "How long was Mr. Singer your assistant?"

"For the last three movies. Two years."

"You have the numbers to contact his family?"

"No, I don't. You know, really, I have no idea."

"You do not know his family?"

"Listen, I just worked with the guy on a few projects. His mom and dad never came up. He made reservations for me at restaurants, stuff like that."

Captain Mejzlik rose and went to the door, resting his hand on the knob. He seemed out of breath. "So if you work with someone you don't have a responsibility to get to know his family?"

"Listen, *I* don't know how to get a hold of them, but we can call Jerome at the set and he can probably tell you."

Captain Mejzlik opened the door. "Pitr," he called.

Timothy examined his fingernails.

A young man strode in, his reddish hair combed sideways across his head. He stood at attention as Captain Mejzlik shut the door.

"Now pay attention to this please, Mr. Carson. Witness the difference between the Czech Republic and San Francisco."

Timothy swiveled his chair, the heels of his shoes brushing the pink carpet.

"Pitr, your mother's name is Lida. What is my mother's name?"

"Lujza Mejzlikova."

"My father?"

"Jan Mejzlik."

"And your father is Vaclav Malek."

"Just as you, Captain, have a brother named Vaclav."

"Indeed I do, and you a brother named Antonin."

Timothy stood up and went to the window. He looked down

toward the Charles Bridge and tried to pinpoint where they had been standing when the accident happened. He couldn't see the intersection because of a tower at the foot of the bridge, resplendent with flags and saints. Terrance was in a hospital somewhere in a metal box. It had been a long day for both of them. The sun was low in the sky. Moss grew on the window sill.

"My wife?"

"Lucka, of course!"

"Forgive me, that was an easy one. How about her brother?"

"Plitcha. Plitcha Sinderka."

"Yes, Plitcha Sinderka. Decent fellow."

A policeman drove Timothy up a series of winding lanes to the castle. Stopped at a corner, Timothy saw the jazz singer again, reading a newspaper in a doorway. As they rolled away the man again slid his glasses down and winked at Timothy.

The officer driving had seen it too. "You have to watch out for men like that," he told Timothy. "We don't know what to do with them."

"You speak very good English," said Timothy.

"As does everyone in Prague."

They pulled up in front of the castle, where a throng of tourists stood watching the sunset, showing each other postcards and drinking bottles of lemonade.

Timothy nodded to the officer. "Thanks a lot." He got out and shut the door.

The officer rolled down the passenger window. "I'm sorry about your friend," he said. "But we all must make sacrifices to get what we want. As a famous person you must understand this." He nodded, put the car into neutral and rolled silently down the hill.

Timothy smoothed down his suit jacket and went up the half-dozen steps to the castle gate. A teenaged girl with braces and knee socks came up to him.

"A-aren't you Timothy Carson?" she asked.

He stopped in mid-step and turned to her, brushing back his bangs.

"Why yes, I am," he said. "Who might you be?"

Everyone had turned to look. "B-Belinda Spoor," she said. "I thought it was great in *Nation of Anger* when you threw that garbage can through the principal's window. It, it was so funny."

"Thank you, Belinda," said Timothy. "Thanks a lot." He started back up the steps but then turned and threw his hand over his head, offering an all-encompassing wave to the crowd. Someone took a picture.

In the courtyard another group of tourists watched the changing of the guard come to an end. A dozen men in blue uniforms and tall black hats, rifles over their shoulders, goose-stepped into their barracks through a doorway beside the main gate, their faces fixed in grimaces. A door shut behind them and there was scattered applause.

Timothy pushed through the crowd to reach a gate leading to the next courtyard, farther inside the castle walls. An olive-skinned woman with a gauze of dark hair across her cheeks stood guarding the gate. She held a clipboard and spoke into a headset.

"I haven't eaten. Don't let them go."

Then she saw Timothy and flicked the microphone under her chin. In the failing light both of their faces seemed green.

"My God," she said. "To which hospital have they taken him? This is the worst thing that could have happened! Mr. Bendiner has been on the telephone all afternoon — I think he is trying to get Christian Slater for the part. And you are the only one with numbers for Timothy's family — where have you been? You must go in and see Mr. Bendiner, because if Christian Slater does not come we might as well go back to the U.S. right now. Though of course I'm from Prague, so I would stay here."

"Minka," said Timothy, "you're fucked. A car hit *Terrance*. He died. *I'm* Timothy Carson."

"Mr. Carson," she said. "I misunderstood."

"Did they shoot anything? What happened?"

"They made a change in the schedule and did the scene where the queen smashes her mirror."

"I should see Jerome."

"No, let someone else tell him first. He will be angry about Christian Slater."

Timothy went down a corridor between the high castle walls. Technicians wearing tool belts danced past each other carrying coils of cable over their shoulders. Some nodded to Timothy as he passed them. He watched their hands: calloused for the most part, some wearing Band-Aids and some with black nails, but not one was missing a pinky finger. Near the end of the passage he stopped a man with a huge black moustache, stooped under the weight of a prop door. He had all of his fingers.

"Excuse me," Timothy said slowly. "Where do you come from?"

"What do you mean? I'm from L.A. just like you. In fact, my apartment was right under yours out in Laurel Canyon. You had that girlfriend who did aerobics in the middle of the damn night. Four years ago."

"That's what I thought," said Timothy.

In the courtyard at the centre of the castle sat catering trucks, tall light standards and metal trailers with green doors. Timothy rapped at the door of the largest trailer and went in. There was a light on above the kitchen sink. Jerome Bendiner lay on the leather sofa, his head propped against one end and his bare feet sticking out over the other. He had a bald head and trousers held up with suspenders. There was a blue washcloth across his eyes.

"Tell me who's there," said Jerome.

"The walking wounded," said Timothy.

Jerome did not stir. "Are you hurt badly?"

"It got Terrance. Car never touched me. Sorry today's shooting never happened."

"Old Terrance, he shouldn't have gone out on a day like today. He never ate his breakfast and he told me he hardly slept at all, he was up half the night. Old Terrance. That's a problem. That's a bitch."

Timothy took a bottle of Budvar out of the fridge. The orange-and-white label was wet and slid off in his hand. Jerome rearranged the washcloth over his eyes.

"Jerome, do you want a beer?"

"No thanks, no. Shoot, Terrance and I were going to play a game of golf when we got back. We were looking out at that park over behind the castle and Terrance said if the hillside wasn't so steep it'd be good for a round of golf. Neither one of us had any clubs."

"I didn't know you knew Terrance." Timothy was looking through the drawers for a bottle opener.

"Oh, yeah. Shoot, I've known him for years. He was around when I was putting together *Our September* and some other project, some thing that didn't pay off. A lot of the ladies thought Terrance was pretty charming, you know, but somehow, somehow he could never manage to get anywhere." Jerome rolled onto his side to face Timothy, pulling the washcloth up onto the side of his head. "My secretary, she liked him. I got her a seat when I was nominated for that Oscar and she asked if she could bring Terrance along. But we didn't have enough seats. My wife even invited Terrance to Michael's bar mitzvah, my eldest son Michael. Terrance bought him a catcher's mitt. I don't know how he knew Michael wanted one. Michael was up there doing his recitation and I could see Terrance's lips moving the whole time. He still knew the whole thing from the looks of it. Old Terrance."

Timothy pulled at his beer. "I didn't know you were Jewish, Jerome."

"Yeah."

Timothy toyed with the cord for the venetian blinds, pulling them up the window and letting them slide back down again.

"Hollywood was started by Jewish guys," said Jerome. "Whole movie industry. It was just a nice place in the desert before that. Vacation spot, like Palm Springs. They put their heads together and got it all going and now look at it. Billions of dollars every year. I mean, if you're in L.A. and you're in the industry, you might as well be Jewish. Even if you weren't to start with."

"You think so?"

"Sure."

"Minka told me you thought I was dead."

"She got it wrong. I've already talked with Terrance's sister in Red Hook for an hour."

"I'm going to grab some dinner and pack it in." Timothy set his empty bottle on top of the fridge, where an army of them already stood.

"Why don't you take tomorrow off? We didn't make any headway with Helen. You could probably use the rest."

"I think *you* could use the rest, Jerome."

Minka sat down next to Timothy with a plate of scrambled eggs. She playfully kicked the leg of his folding chair as she chewed.

"What are you sitting out here for?" she said.

Timothy was eating toast. He chewed and swallowed. "Waiting for the changing of the guard."

Minka nodded. "I like to watch it. Of course, they are dressed as fools, but it makes me feel safe. The nice little Czech army."

"And not the Russians."

"Or Germans."

"You remember Germans?" Timothy asked. "I thought that was ages ago."

"Not me, but my parents do. My mother always talks about it."

The courtyard was empty, the gate still locked, the cobblestones glistening with dew. The door in the gatehouse opened and one of the blue-coated guards came out. He waved to Minka with a rag and she waved back, then he sat against the wall and began polishing his boots.

"During the war," Minka said, "my grandparents hid a refugee. He was Jewish, a businessman, I think. His family had escaped a long time before, but he wanted to stay behind. I think he worked with my grandfather. My grandfather wanted to get him into the countryside, but he refused to leave Prague. Even though German tanks rolled in the street every day and he had to wear a star on his clothes, he would not leave. Then the Nazis began to arrest the Jews. They came to where he lived and he said he shot one of the Nazis while they were arresting him. He got away and came to our house. A few days later they came to our house looking for him. Over the years they came many times. They tapped on the walls and broke through the floor, but they could never find him. They expected him to hide somewhere difficult, but he was just in the bottom of the china cabinet. Every day he would get out and stretch for a few minutes, and then he would get back in. He was rolled up in there like a tiny ball. One day my mother and my grandparents came home and found him stretched out on the floor. He had shot himself in the head. My grandmother was sure the Nazis had done it and made it look like suicide. But if you've seen any movies with Nazis in them, you know they would not have left him there. They would have taken him back to their officer and said, 'Sir, we have killed this Jew,' and the officer would have responded, 'Excellent job, men, Heil Hitler!' So my grandfather never believed that the Nazis had killed him, he said that his friend had come out of the cabinet and could not bring himself to go back in. But my grandparents were in just as much danger with the man's corpse still in the house, so they waited until the middle of the night and dragged it to a street corner a mile away. And the Nazis still came back, but with the man out of the house it was almost funny to watch them knocking on things and looking under the bed. Once my mother even burst out laughing."

"Your eggs are cold, Minka."

"Oh, that's all right," she said and scooped a forkful off her plate. "What about your family? Weren't any of them in the war?"

"My grandpa fought the Japanese," said Timothy. "But he didn't ever talk about it. Nothing to tell, I guess."

Minka scraped up the rest of the egg with her fork.

The guard had finished polishing his boots and now stood beside the gate with a few others. An officer with a cup of coffee in his hand came out of the gatehouse and blew a whistle and the guards began doing jumping jacks.

"What do you remember about the Russians?" asked Timothy.

She smiled at him. "I remember when they left. I was watching out a window with my brothers and about one hundred of their soldiers were marching in the square, down by the clock tower, you know where I mean? All of these soldiers and all so quiet."

"Was there fighting?"

"No. The radio had been shut down, but then it came back

on and said 'Independence! Revolution!' or some such thing, so my brothers and I went down to a bar. By this time it was evening and the soldiers were all just standing around in the street with their guns. Anything could have happened. We walked by the soldiers and went in for a beer. The people in the bar began dancing and singing and at midnight the soldiers came in and had drinks too and everyone patted them on the back. One of the Russians was drunk and started to kiss me. He was showing his gun to everyone and just before we went home one of my brothers' friends was shot by his girlfriend."

The guards stood at attention as the officer opened the gate. A tour bus was visible outside.

"I should get to work," said Minka, rising. "Give me your dish."

Timothy handed her his plate and she disappeared into the castle. He stood up and stretched his arms high above his head, then bent down to touch his toes. Then up to stretch his arms again.

He crossed the courtyard and went down the steps to where a tour guide was pointing out the features of the outer wall. The bus pulled away from the sidewalk, revealing the jazz singer of the day before, leaning against a lamppost across the street, eating a roll. As he caught sight of Timothy he took off his bowler hat and shook it in the air, chewing all the while. He had a thick head of black hair.

Timothy crossed the street. As he approached, the man continued shaking the hat, lowering it until it was in front of his stomach.

"Timothy Carson," said the man, "the famous movie star."

"Maybe in the States," said Timothy.

"Oh, we know you here," said the man, replacing his hat. "We know you." He brought his hand down and Timothy saw that it consisted of a thumb and three fingers. The knuckle of his pinky finger was wrapped in gauze. Timothy stared at it.

"People love my finger. It never did heal properly," said the man, blowing on the bandage. "My name is Karel. Now come with me, I want to discuss your films."

"*Sabotage*," said Karel, "was a great film. Your best. You played the part very well. It is a memorable performance in a great film."

"I agree," said Timothy, his face in a glass of beer.

The tavern was empty except for him and Karel and a couple of middle-aged ladies sitting at the bar having coffee. The waitress polished each of the liquor bottles on the wall and sang softly to herself. It was a very clean establishment.

"But *Murdering Mr. Hobbs* was your worst film."

"I don't want to talk about *Murdering Mr. Hobbs*."

"Yes, *Murdering Mr. Hobbs* was your biggest mistake," said Karel. "I imagine it was supposed to be a screwball comedy or the like, like that film at the summer camp, what was that? *Meatballs*."

"*Meatballs*," repeated Timothy.

"Yes, but *Meatballs* had Bill Murray. It was a smallish part I know, but he brought to the film a sort of kinetic energy. Now in *Murdering Mr. Hobbs* you were the straight man and that would have been fine had they cast a Bill Murray or even a Nicolas Cage next to you. But there was no one. It was a whole cast of straight men and as a consequence any hope for humour in the film died a quick and pitiful death."

Timothy set his glass down on the wooden table and licked his lips. "Everyone says Ivan Reitman is a genius anyway."

"That they do," said Karel, nodding. "That they do."

"*Ghostbusters*."

"Yes, *Ghostbusters*," said Karel. "With the marshmallow man." He took a pack of cigarettes out of his pocket and passed one to Timothy.

"Or *Stripes*. He's a genius," said Timothy.

"*Stripes*! My God, yes!"

"Or *Dave*, did you see that one? Kevin Kline's in it."

"*Dave*. That is the film where Kevin Kline works for an employment agency and is able to impersonate the president and seduce the president's wife. He convinces everyone that he is someone he is not."

"Well, yeah." Timothy pulled on his cigarette. "But he was a good-hearted guy to begin with. He didn't do anything wrong."

"But he kept it a secret and that can make people assume the worst." Karel took a long drink from his glass of beer, set it down, took off his tinted glasses and began to clean them on his shirt-tail. He had massive bags under his eyes. "For example, Mr. Carson, several times in the 1980s myself and every member of our little music group were arrested and imprisoned. It was because we were regularly meeting in private. The police didn't like it."

"They assumed the worst," said Timothy, tapping ash into his empty glass.

"Of course they did. They assumed we were planning a secret militia right there in the kitchen of Vilem's house. You might have seen Vilem with us yesterday, when you passed by. He plays the trombone. We were there at his house, playing 'Swinging on a Star,' I think, and a few men came in the door and put us in handcuffs. We insisted, I'm sure you can imagine, that we were only musicians practising. They even said that this was a good attempt to deceive them, but not nearly good enough. As they put me in the back of a car I was told it was the worst rendition of 'Swinging on a Star' any of them had ever heard."

Timothy leaned back in his chair and put his hands behind his head.

"You too, Mr. Carson, would have had to be careful here during those days," said Karel. "If the authorities had watched

Murdering Mr. Hobbs they would have said to themselves, 'This is not a film. What are those hooligans planning?'" Karel laughed, tipping his head back, then picked up their empty glasses and went to the bar. When he returned Timothy had his head in his hands.

"Don't blame me for *Murdering Mr. Hobbs*," said Timothy. "My agent thought I should try comedy and he said the director was so into coke I wouldn't have to audition. I have to confess. I wasn't supposed to be the straight man. They thought I could be funny."

Karel pushed a full beer under Timothy's chin. "Then it is time to stop hiding from yourself. You are not in the least bit funny."

The waitress came over and put her hand on Timothy's shoulder. She had a thin arm and wore a white T-shirt.

"I knew it," she said. "I knew it. You are Timothy Carson."

Karel said he wanted to show Timothy some sights. They wandered back over the Charles Bridge and stood waiting at the intersection where Terrance had been killed — right at the spot where his body had landed.

"A friend of mine was killed right here," said Timothy.

"When was that? With the Communists?"

"It was yesterday."

"What, that fellow you were walking with?"

"That was him."

"Here and then so quickly gone. At least you will not forget him."

The signal changed and they walked across. A breeze blew up from the river.

"Where are we going?"

"I want to take you to the Jewish cemetery in Josefov," said Karel. "It is breathtaking. Twenty thousand graves."

"Are you Jewish, Karel?"

"No. Are you?"

"I don't know. I've been told I have a Jewish name."

"Carson is not a Jewish name."

"Klapka is my real name."

It was still midmorning and the streets were empty. They passed only one vendor, standing beside a steaming pot and a cardboard sign reading GROG. As they walked through the square where Timothy had first seen Karel, the clock tower began to strike the hour. A few teenagers in shorts started snapping pictures. As the bells tolled, ceramic skeletons on either side of the clock's face began to dance eerily, though they did not dance so much as stand in place and shake their bones.

"Let's see if the rabbi is at home."

Timothy stood under a great flowering tree as Karel tapped at the iron side door of the caretaker's house. The cemetery itself did not cover much ground, perhaps a single city block. But from the low front wall to the lichen-covered wall at the back, nothing could be seen but gravestones. They were stacked against one another, fifteen and twenty thick, so that, had the gravestones been a uniform height, they might have resembled a paved surface. But many had crumbled into piles of rubble, some were tall and broad and others were short, squat posts; all that they had in common was the rough grey rock they'd been hewn from. Timothy leaned over the front wall to read the letters on the nearest gravestones, but only the barest impressions lingered. The names had been eroded, dusted with yellow moss.

"Timothy, come on," said Karel. The door was opening. Karel and Timothy ducked under the lintel to step inside.

The rabbi's quarters were surprisingly bright. Fluorescent

lights lined the low cement walls, revealing stacks of ancient-looking books and a collection of tattered wooden furniture. Their host shut the door and nodded at them. He was of medium height, dressed all in black, wearing a broad-brimmed black hat and a long black coat that brushed the carpet. He had a red beard and long sidelocks dangling beside his ears. He gestured for them to sit. Timothy's chair creaked as though surprised.

"David Hayim," Karel said to Timothy, his broad bandaged hand indicating the rabbi, who nodded quickly.

"*Zdravstvuite*," said David Hayim.

"He speaks English," said Karel.

"Oh. Do you?" said David Hayim. "I see."

"My name's Timothy Carson. I'm from America." He glanced at Karel. "I'm an actor."

"Are you? That's very interesting." The rabbi turned one of the chairs around and straddled it, leaning his chest against its wooden back.

"I wanted him to see the graves," said Karel.

"Yes, they are very nice, very nice," said David Hayim. "You could make a movie about them. Might be a fun time."

"You could make twenty thousand movies," said Karel. "Every one of those graves — and how the occupant came to be in it — could be the subject of a feature film."

"It sure could," said Timothy. "Those would be *films*."

"But don't dig any up, all right?" David Hayim leaned forward and gave Timothy a playful slap on the knee. He suddenly pointed at Karel. "What kind of host am I? Do you want biscuits?"

"No thanks, Rabbi," said Karel.

"We just ate," said Timothy.

"Glass of tea?"

"No thanks."

"Carrots?"

"We're fine," said Timothy. "Thank you."

"Fruit juice?"

"No."

"Okay," said David Hayim. He snapped his fingers. "What kind of movies are you in?"

"We're making one up at the castle. It's about this prince who gives up his throne to wander the countryside. He fights a dragon."

"And an evil person takes the throne," said the rabbi, "and the people suffer and the prince returns to fight the villain and become king. I see."

"You know the story," said Timothy.

The rabbi waved his hand. "Everyone knows that story."

"You could make it one of your films for the cemetery," said Karel. "You could have the prince be buried here. You could end the film with a shot of his grave with people in modern dress walking by with shopping bags and things. It would show his place in history, though his stone has been worn blank."

"Karel," said Timothy, "that could really work."

"He would have to be a Jewish prince," said the rabbi.

"That could really work," Timothy said.

"What other movies have you been in?" said David Hayim.

"Timothy was in *Sabotage*," said Karel.

"*Sabotage*?" said the rabbi. "That is a great movie. I enjoyed that. I see. But you know who is great? Karel. You should hear him." David Hayim waggled his fingers in the air, as though he were playing a clarinet. He gave Karel a broad smile.

"I've heard him," said Timothy. "He's great."

The rabbi nodded and smiled. With two fingers he tapped a beat on the back of his chair.

"Rabbi," said Timothy, "you must know a lot about the Jews."

David Hayim raised his eyebrows and continued tapping.

Karel looked at his wristwatch and rose from his chair. "It's time I met the others. Vilem has a new song. Do you want to stay with the rabbi?"

"I'd like to," said Timothy. "Is that okay?"

"Oh. Oh, of course," said the rabbi. "Please."

"Thanks for showing me around," said Timothy. "I'll probably see you tonight."

"It will be a pleasure," said Karel. He rubbed the back of his neck and went out, ducking his head beneath the doorframe.

"Rabbi," said Timothy, leaning forward on his elbows. "Is Klapka a Jewish name?"

"Klapka? Yes. Maybe. Certainly. It could be a Jewish name."

"What do you mean?"

"Well. You see, it's like the name Kafka. You know the Czech writer Kafka?"

"No."

"The Czech writer Kafka was a Jew, so many people think of Kafka as a Jewish name. You see? But it is just a Czech name. He happened to have that name and he happened to be a Jew."

"How's that possible?"

"Oh, well. Over the years many Jews have changed their Hebrew names, or they have married Christians. Now one's name does not mean so much. You see? Especially in America. Many, many Jews who arrived in America changed their names. In America a man could be a Jew and be named Ronald Reagan."

"My name is really Klapka. Timothy Klapka."

"It is? Ha ha ha." David Hayim's mouth fell open as he laughed, exposing his broad white teeth.

"What? What?"

"I am sorry. It is just funny. The name sounds funny. It is a good name. Is it Jewish?"

"That's what I'm asking you!"

"Oh. I see. All right then, it's Jewish if you want it to be. Do you want it to be Jewish?"

"Sort of," said Timothy.

"Why is that?"

"Well, Carson doesn't mean anything," said Timothy. "Klapka, you know, it's got guts."

"Would it still have guts if it were not a Jewish name?" The rabbi frowned deliberately, as though to underline the gravity of the question.

"Not so many guts." Timothy nodded. "Being Jewish is gutsy."

"And a Jew is what you want to be."

"I think so, yeah. It's who I am."

The rabbi stretched out his legs. He wore argyle socks. "You should come to synagogue, then, Mr. Klapka. Before long we could hold your bar mitzvah."

"Oh, I'm circumcised already," said Timothy.

"That's wonderful news." The rabbi stared at Timothy and pulled at his lower lip with a thumb and forefinger. Then he pushed against the chair and stood up. "I'll put the samovar on for tea." He left the room.

Timothy sat with his hands on his knees and forced his mouth into a wry smile. He felt somehow ashamed, as though he had just made a pass at the rabbi. He felt excited, tingling, yet ashamed.

"Rabbi, do you have a telephone?" He got up and followed David Hayim.

The rabbi was putting a huge brass kettle on his stove. "No. There is a telephone on the street."

Timothy felt in his pockets. "What does it take, a crown?"

"It needs a phonecard. Here, take mine." The rabbi unbuttoned his coat and took a blue plastic phonecard out of the pocket of his white shirt. He handed it to Timothy.

"How does it work?"

"I'll come with you," said David Hayim.

Outside the wind was blowing blossoms from the flowering tree across the cemetery. Pink and red petals, caught in eddies of the breeze, circled around the gravestones, spiralling to the earth only to be caught up again. A cascade of blossoms blew up into their faces, settling on Timothy's shoulders and catching in the rabbi's beard.

Timothy picked up the telephone receiver.

"Here, here. First." The rabbi took the phonecard from Timothy and slid it into the top of the keypad. Some numbers came up on a tiny display screen. "Okay. It's okay. I hope you are not calling Phnom Penh."

"I'm just phoning up to the castle." Timothy typed in a number.

"Oh, the castle. Very smart. How do you know the phone number there?"

"It's my producer's cellular." It began ringing at the other end.

"Oh, a cellular. I see. Very smart. You are a smart actor."

"Thanks."

"Hello?" It was a woman's voice on the line.

"Hello, Jerome?" said Timothy.

"This is not Jerome. This is Kathy speaking. This is a private line for Mr. Bendiner's calls. Who's speaking please?"

"Just let me speak with Jerome, Kathy. Tell him it's Timothy."

David Hayim leaned his head against the side of the phone box, pressing the brim of his hat into his face.

"Timothy who?"

"Just tell him I'm on the line, Kathy! Jesus Christ, would you just go tell him?"

"He may be indisposed, sir. I'll have to see if I can find him."

"Could you? That'd be *great*." Timothy set the receiver on his shoulder. "Hey, Rabbi."

"Yes?" The rabbi's voice was muffled behind his hat.

"Later on can we see if there are any other Klapkas who live in Prague? I'd like to see if they're Jewish. Maybe they're my relatives."

"We'll see," said David Hayim.

"Hello?" Jerome's voice spoke into Timothy's shoulder.

Timothy put the phone to his ear. "Hey, Jerome? It's Timothy."

"Timothy, this day is like a, is like a nightmare. Helen cut her damn hand on the mirror and got blood on that lace get-up we got over in England. I'd like to stop this movie and start over."

"Hey, Jerome, tell the marketing guys I'm going to want a change. I don't want it to say Carson on the posters anymore. I want it to say Klapka."

"What the hell?"

"It's my real name, Jerome. It's a Jewish name. Like Bendiner."

"This is a godawful waste of time. Why make a joke about this?"

The pink and red blossoms blew in a dust devil across the pavement.

"Look, Jerome, just fire me if it turns out this is a joke. Don't pay me anything. I'm not jerking you around, I really want my name to say Timothy Klapka."

"That's stupid. So the TV ads will say, 'Starring Timothy Klapka,' and the people at home'll say 'Who the fuck is that? Hey, when's Timothy Carson's new film coming out? I love that guy.' No way, Timothy. Not on any picture of mine."

"Look, fuck you, Jerome. I'll do what I want all right? You can shove your movie right where I know you like it, I don't need your crap. I'm gonna stay in Prague anyway — there are more important things than your fucking movie."

The rabbi's hand shot out and pulled the phone away from Timothy's ear. His head was still pressed against the side of the phone box.

"Hello, Jerome?" said the rabbi.

"Who the fuck is this?"

"This is Reb David Hayim speaking. I am a friend of Mr. Carson's. I wanted you to know, sir, that he hasn't any intention of staying in Prague and would like to return home as soon as possible. He will cooperate for the completion of your film and would like to know if there is anything he can do to help you."

"Tell Timothy to get up here."

"Thank you." The rabbi hung up the receiver. "You are to go back. The boss says so."

"What are you talking about?" asked Timothy. "I'm not going back to that idiot."

"Yes, you will," said David Hayim. His sidelocks fluttered in the wind. "You have escaped. You cannot stay here. Go back to America. Do not expect us to have memories for you. Go on, enjoy yourself. Have a good time." He patted Timothy on the arm. "My samovar will boil."

Timothy stood with his arms at his sides as the rabbi went down the path to his house. Timothy looked out across the graves. He felt all of history regard him with disgust.

After a moment the rabbi came back out of his house, crossed the street and stopped in front of him. Timothy folded his arms. The rabbi pulled his card out of the phone, nodded to him, and turned back to his house. Timothy watched his neat figure disappear through the door.

In a house nearby someone began to play trombone.

BEAUTIFUL FEET

*And how can they preach unless they are
sent? As it is written, "How beautiful are the
feet of those who bring good news!"*

Romans 10:15

ONE

Melissa twisted in her seat and tried to crack her neck,
pulling her shoulder blades back and turning her head
sharply to one side. Just as the vertebrae gave a satisfying
pop she had her first glimpse of the Philippines out the window
of the plane.

She knew it was Luzon Island they were over, eight hundred
kilometres long, and she gazed down on it for a while before saying
anything to the others. It looked like a movie about medieval
England, she thought: patches of rolling fog, sleepy valleys
and houses clustered on the tops of stunted hills. The land was

carpeted with green turf, over the ridges and alongside the rivers, like moss over an ancient skeleton. She pictured feudal peasants trudging up those hills, carrying their enemies' heads and shivering. It looked cold down on the ground, because of the fog, not unlike the autumn day in Vancouver they had just left behind.

She watched the hills drop away to flatter country, where the clusters of houses spread out into towns. Soon the pilot would be announcing Manila.

Barney was asleep in the seat next to her. Their sixteen-year-old son Graeme sat in the aisle seat, wearing his new dress shirt with the button-down collar. He had put down his Bible and was reading the in-flight magazine, holding it open to a full-page picture of a Filipina girl in a white bikini. He turned the page, then back to the bikini. The girl in the picture had small breasts and this pleased Melissa. She didn't want him to limit his options.

She entwined her fingers with Barney's, soft with sleep. Whenever anyone had doubted their ability to see the project through, Barney had claimed that he was ready for any situation. This extended to riding in an airplane: their situation required sleep so that he'd be rested for what lay ahead. He didn't take meals. He did nothing. He slept. Every time she stepped over his legs to get to the bathroom, he would give her a dirty look.

He had a wide face with thin lips, but his jaw was strong and he had a moustache. He looked a little like Clark Gable, a woman from the congregation had told her, and sometimes she could see it in his profile. Melissa was tall and slender and straight, and her blonde hair, in a ponytail now, was straight as well. It had been curly until one day in high school when she'd ironed it, and it had been straight as a rod ever since. She'd been wilder with curly hair, people said, and she liked it that she'd been wild.

She took Barney's chin and turned his head toward her. His eyes opened to look her in the face and then immediately past her, through the window. She watched them narrow as they focused on what lay below.

"They put some Philippines down there for us," Melissa said. She bumped her forehead gently against his.

"Looks like farms," said Barney. "Where's the jungle?"

"There were mountains before."

"These people look like they're fine. Isn't that white thing a church?"

Graeme hovered in his aisle seat, trying to see out the window too. Melissa tucked a hair behind her ear and smiled at him.

"Well, if anybody needs to hear the good news, tell them just to wait for us," Barney said. He flopped back against the seat and shook Graeme's knee, digging his thumb and fingers in. "Almost, my boy, almost, hey?"

Graeme jerked his leg away. She often saw that look on his face, as though his eyes were about to tear up, as though his features hadn't meshed enough to form a face at all. It was his age. She knew that part of him was excited about the trip, because he'd taken sharp breaths as they'd stood in line with their boarding passes. But a larger part of him didn't want to be prodded by his father or carried around the Philippines in a backpack like he had been at Expo 86 when he was two years old.

Melissa and Barney went to the Youth Group meeting because Barney was one of the leaders. Graeme was obviously a youth, but he didn't go this time because Wally Bonin's dad had just been killed at the loading docks and a bunch of Wally's friends were going over to visit. But when she and Barney came home early from the meeting, they found Graeme and a girl standing in the living room, smelling of the hot tub, their hair soaking wet. They'd never seen the girl before. She had a small frame and braces and her choice of bra made her breasts look pointy. The hot tub had been a fifteenth-anniversary gift — a gift of encouragement — from Melissa's mother.

"This is Linda," said Graeme. "It was raining. We came in for hot chocolate."

But there were no dirty mugs.

They asked Linda if she would need a ride home, but she said that a friend was picking her up. The car that came was full of kids and the ones in the back were smoking. The three of them, the Jordan family, stood on the front walk and watched the car squeal away. Then Barney suggested they go inside and talk about what had happened.

They sat on the sofa, Melissa and Barney, and Graeme sat leaning forward in the easy chair. The only light was from the kitchen.

"We *were* in the hot tub," Graeme said. "But we were already soaking wet, from the rain. It was cold. It's not like anything could have happened—"

"Where's your bathing suit?" asked Barney.

They went into Graeme's room and the suit was sitting folded in the dresser drawer, where it always was, clean and dry. He'd never put it on.

Barney pushed him with both hands. Graeme fell down onto the floor in front of his closet.

The blinds on the round windows of the plane were pushed up, throwing light into the cabin like holes punched in a tin can. Passengers turned off their reading lights and the flight attendants collected blankets.

A stout Filipina woman in a floral blouse got up from the seats ahead of them and opened the overhead compartment. As she stood on tiptoe she glanced up and down the aisle for someone who could help.

Melissa reached across and squeezed Graeme's wrist, motioning with her eyes.

"Give her a hand, Graeme," said Barney.

Graeme got up, nodding as though he'd been going to do it all along.

"Oh, thank you," said the woman. She stepped back and clasped her hands to her chest. "The blue one. At the back."

Graeme handed down a turquoise purse. "You want something else?" he asked.

"Please close it for me," said the woman. He pulled down the door of the bin while the woman fished a pack of Three Musketeers chocolate bars from her bag. She put the purse under her armpit and tore the package open with her teeth.

"Here," she said, picking a scrap of plastic from her lip. "They're for my blood pressure. You know, I forgot to take my pills and I have to have them with food. You take some, for Mama and Papa too." She pressed three of the bars into Graeme's hands.

"No, please. You need those," said Melissa.

The woman shook her head, chewing furiously. Graeme took his seat. The woman pulled chocolate off her teeth with her tongue. "You are from Seattle?"

This flight had left from Seattle. In the transit lounge, Barney had been annoyed with Melissa because he'd wanted to phone some of the elders from the affiliated Christian Workers Fellowship but she'd insisted that there wasn't time.

"We're from Vancouver," said Melissa. "Canada."

"Oh, my brother is in Vancouver, Washington. He is a sailor." She covered her mouth and swallowed a lump of Three Musketeers. "I live in Eugene, Oregon, now but I come back to Manila for Christmas. My daughter is coming from Australia."

"She comes home for Christmas too?"

"Oh, yes." The woman lowered her chin and beamed with pride. "You are coming for holiday?"

"We're going up into the jungle," said Barney, "to plant churches."

"What do you mean? You are missionaries?" She pointed at each of them with the stump of her chocolate bar. "The country is filled with churches! You should go to New Guinea instead. Human sacrifice, they say. My brother has been there. In the Philippines we are all Catholic people."

"The Catholics," said Barney, "say that the good news about Christ can only be handed down by the priest from his pulpit. And *we* say that the word of God is in each person's heart and in the Bible, and to have a church you don't need anything else. You don't need official permission from any pope or bishop." Filipino passengers shifted in the surrounding seats, trying to get a look at him. "You tell people about Jesus and right then and there they plant their church. It's that simple."

The woman dug into her purse for her medicine. "Well, I hope you have some big shovels for the planting!" she said, and smiled. She took out two pills, swallowed them and put the vial back. Then she stood helplessly in the aisle, holding her purse.

"Here," said Graeme. He got to his feet again and opened the compartment.

"Oh, thank you," said the woman. She handed him the bag.

"Graeme," said Barney. "She's all right. Leave it alone."

Graeme lifted the purse beside his head.

"Give it back," said Barney. "Give it back to her."

Graeme paused. He lowered the purse into her hands.

"Now sit."

Graeme took his seat and immediately reached for the in-flight magazine while the other passengers murmured around them. The woman stood with her mouth open, gazing at Barney until she shook her head and sat down with the purse in her lap. A stewardess walked by and shut the overhead compartment.

Barney shifted the money belt under his shirt, stuffed with the traveller's cheques and Filipino pesos it had taken them a year to save, and shut his eyes.

He must think he looks like a saint on a stained-glass window, Melissa thought. Saint Barney of the Seat in the Upright Position.

Melissa was leaning over the office counter using the paper-cutter on the first day of Grade 11, and Barney was new at the school and was seeing her legs and back end for the first time. "I know how to have a pretty good time," he said to her. This was one of the dumbest things she had ever heard.

When she got pregnant, she was working in a coffee shop on the corner of Pender and Seymour. By then they had been going out for three years and Barney was practising hard with the band. He played bass, but was trying to convince the guys that he should be the lead singer.

Their parents were not church people, so they didn't even care if she and Barney got married. They just moved in together, into an upstairs suite at East Eighth and Victoria, an Italian neighbourhood. He contributed the money the band made at parties toward rent, but it wasn't enough, so she took extra shifts at the coffee shop. Coming home from work one night, she sat at the bus stop with a stove burn on the side of her hand and thought of a Christmas morning with kids and stockings and Barney making coffee and bringing it to her.

One Saturday morning she woke up in astounding pain, as if

a pair of scissors were twisting inside her. When she pulled back the covers she found she'd already miscarried. She slid down to the floor and he crawled over to her. He said that they could try again, though they hadn't been trying in the first place, and that they ought to get married. "Nothing else means anything to me," he said, and looked around the room. It struck her then that his feet were long and beautiful. They seemed to represent the many things that were still possible.

"They won't let me sing anyway," he said.

They quit smoking and got married and Barney found a job with the Parks Board. He cut his hair and beard but kept the moustache.

After a few months they sat drinking white wine at a Board potluck and she thought of how, on some of the band's songs, the guitar would come in, then the drums and finally the bass, and how she used to wait for that moment, everyone else already dancing and whooping, but she in the audience and he on the stage, silent, both waiting for that deep, euphoric note. Everything about their new life was watered down by comparison. Once she went to pick him up at Stanley Park and he was standing in a flower bed, mouthing some inaudible song and playing a hoe like it was his bass.

She told her mother that she was probably going to leave Barney. Her mother waved a hand and blew on her wet nail polish.

"It's up to you, of course. But if you do that, you'll never know what might have come next. There's nothing more interesting, if you ask me, than seeing how a couple turns out down the road."

"What if they go on to become new couples with other people?"

"Then they're just repeating themselves."

But then Graeme was born and everything that touched the baby, or was in another part of the house but concerned the baby, or things she saw outside that reminded her of the baby, those things were perfect. Barney loved to pick Graeme up, swing him around, and he loved it, he told her, that when he woke up in the morning it was to two people who needed him.

"Be careful when you go downtown in Manila," shouted the cab driver, "especially if you take Metrorail. There are many pickpockets, you know, because it is Christmas time. You want to buy nice presents for the family, you know what I mean? Thieves too!" He had three plastic Virgin Marys stuck to his dashboard — red, green and blue — and a rosary hung from the rear-view mirror. The ID card next to the meter said Luis Yuson.

The Jordan family sat together in the back seat. Melissa felt buried beneath the humidity, the noise, the pressure of husband and son on either side. The smell of Manila had been in her nostrils since they'd come off the plane, the same overpowering musty smell as when she opened a container of old leftovers. She wanted to get into every kitchen and bathroom and scrub them until the smell went away; that was all this country needed.

"Well, we won't be here long!" Barney shouted.

The car horns were deafening. Eight lanes of traffic converged around them. White cars travelling in packs and big silver buses with decals saying *God's Faithfulness* veered in next to the taxi only to shoot off down an exit, the drivers leaning on their horns. Melissa thought that to stand out a driver ought *not* to lean on his horn. A tiny motorcycle swung in front of them, its passengers, a mother and baby, turned backward to face them. The baby was asleep, its head hanging forward.

At a red light, they looked out at a movie billboard depicting an orange-skinned man with a machine gun and an orange-skinned woman in a leather vest. *Terminator Two.*

Luis stopped sounding his horn. "Manila is a big place," he said. He ran his fingertips over the steering wheel. "It eats up the towns around it. All these kids from villages, too, they fight like hell to get here, to Manila, Manila, Manila, and then they get eaten up too."

"Chews you up and spits you out," said Barney.

"No, it doesn't," said Luis. He turned to face them. "It swallows you alive, so you live next to its heart and suffocate." He faced forward and touched one of his Marys on the head. To their left was the ocean and a few thin old men with fishing rods. The trunks of the palm trees were black with pollution.

"But you want to go to the beach," Luis continued. "Boracay, right? Plane tickets are cheap now. We go to a travel agent. I know one over on Roxas."

"We're going to 328 Dumarao Street," snapped Barney. "That's the only place we want to go."

"All these buses," said Melissa. "Are they decorated for Christmas?"

"They always look like that!" shouted Luis. He wrestled the taxi into first gear and the traffic charged beneath the green light. "You're going to see friends?"

"A colleague," said Barney. "A business colleague."

"You might want to wait for us when we get there," Graeme said, his voice shaking. "We don't know for sure he'll even be there or where we're supposed to go. We might have to get back to the airport."

A bus with huge, angry-looking Japanese writing on its side went by the taxi, its passengers peering down at them through tinted glass, its horn sounding.

"What did you say?" shouted Luis.

None of them answered. Barney rolled his window the rest of the way down to let in some air.

143

Their congregation met on Sunday mornings in a classroom in the Christian elementary school, and the main talk each week was given by Bob Watson or Harry Egan or Harry's wife, Lynn. Harry had a crew cut and wire-rimmed glasses. When he was in his twenties he had gone on a mission up the Amazon River, planting churches and putting Jesus into needy hearts, and most of his talks drew on these missionary days. It was easy to picture him there, looking the same except for a khaki shirt and shorts and the dark, dripping jungle all around him.

"The people were living in mud huts that were never dry. The children were all sick, with welts on their mouths and eyes. I tried to give them medicine, but they didn't trust me. For weeks and weeks I practised speaking with them, going about my business, earning their trust. Eventually, I was able to give them medicine and a long time after that I was able to talk to them about Christ. And when the snake bit my arm I got some medicine in return, didn't I? That's a *great* story."

Usually the talk would end with Matthew 28:19: "Go and make disciples of all nations, baptizing them in the name of the Father and of the Son and of the Holy Spirit." It made for a strong finish, especially if the point of the talk was to encourage the teenagers to tell their friends at school about Jesus. How could anybody hear about Harry's feats and still be too shy to talk to the kid at the next locker?

But Harry had not done his work alone. Time and again he had turned to his overseer, Mr. Thomas, for spiritual guidance, for translation and once even for ammunition. There were a number of missionaries along that stretch of the Amazon and Mr. Thomas puttered between them in a dilapidated tugboat. Sometimes he would chastise Harry if his teaching was going astray, but more often he would put an arm around him as though they were the only believers on Earth. Mr. Thomas shared that moment with everyone on the river; he was St. Paul and they the Corinthians.

"I'm the Christian I am today," Harry said, "because of Mr. Thomas." And no one could deny that Harry was an exceptionally good Christian. "Where is Mr. Thomas now?" everyone asked. Well, Mr. Thomas was heading a mission project in the Philippines now. He was in Manila.

Outside the windows of the taxi, vendors strolled the pavement selling meat on sticks. There was a 7-Eleven store, with a security guard, surrounded by wooden shacks patched up with tin and cardboard. The smell of hot garbage was so strong that Melissa could feel it on the roof of her mouth.

Two small boys stood naked in a plastic tub on the sidewalk, taking turns pouring water over each other's head. A bent woman stood in the entrance of the nearest shack with a black-and-red chicken under her arm.

Most shacks had the name of the family handwritten beside the door — Adriano, Sarmiento — just as families in Canada hung wooden signs on their carports.

"Son," said Barney, "I think that for the good of the project you ought to speak only to your mother or me."

"Do we know what we're doing?" asked Graeme. "Aren't we going to need stuff? Like a translator?"

"This country was a United States colony from 1898 to 1947," said Barney. He rolled the window back up in agitation. "Everybody speaks English."

"Then isn't everybody already Christian?" asked Graeme. This came out louder and angrier than he had probably intended.

Melissa remembered when Barney had used the mixing board to get the levels just right, back in his days with the band; Graeme needed one now.

"Here's 328," said Luis. He stopped the cab.

Barney was out in an instant and Melissa followed him. Women and chickens stopped what they were doing to stare. One little girl stood only a few feet from the taxi, her hair frizzed out like a halo. She was not wearing any pants or underpants, only a T-shirt that said *Anchor Milk New Zealand*, with a picture of an anchor.

"Hello, lamb," said Melissa. She put a hand into her purse for some change, as she would for a panhandler on Granville Street, but then she remembered that they were missionaries now and that handing out money was something they did not do. The little girl looked expectantly at the purse. Melissa pulled out a pair of sunglasses and put them on.

"Whas your name?" asked the little girl.

Melissa felt something rise in her throat and she hurried a few steps to where Luis was unloading luggage. She wondered if every white person felt as awkward as she did. Luis looked at her over his shoulder.

Number 328 was an old building, three stories high, with fake columns built into the front. The logo of the CWF, the Christian Workers Fellowship, was over the door: a pair of out-stretched hands that resembled a dove in flight. The Jordans each had a polo shirt with it emblazoned on the chest.

The building had two dozen windows facing the street and taped up in each was a different poster of Jesus and his crown of thorns, a close-up of his face, painted by a child. The effect was of being scrutinized by rows of severed heads. There was a lot of blood on each Jesus and she imagined the children commiserating over his sufferings as they mixed up another tablet of red paint.

"Is there an art class here?" Graeme asked.

"No, Graeme," said Barney. He was paying Luis the fare. "As long as we're here, *you're* the teacher. You remember that."

Luis put the money in his pants pocket.

"Well, let's see what they've got for us," said Barney. "Let's see, let's see."

A Filipino man leapt up from behind a desk to help them as they banged through the front doors. He wore a short-sleeved dress shirt and a cheaply made CWF baseball cap. The foyer was two stories high, with staircases curving up either side to the upper floors. Everything was painted a lacklustre green. The smell of cooking fish was heavy in the air.

"Hi, hi," he said. "You fly in today for missionary work? Good for you!"

"We have. That's right." They stacked the luggage on a table.

"I'm Jorge," he said, extending a hand. "What time is your appointment?"

"We're here to see Mr. Thomas," said Barney. "Name's Jordan. I'm Barney. This is Melissa. This is Graeme. Very excited."

"We haven't got an appointment, though," said Melissa.

"Oh, you see he's busy at this time," said Jorge. "Without an appointment he can't be seen."

"Well, we're ready to do the good work," said Barney. "What can I tell you?"

A young man in a tie glared down at them from the second floor.

Graeme leaned on a pile of bundled leaflets, his mouth half open and his eyes nearly shut. The same feeling of exhaustion pulled itself over Melissa like a blanket.

"I'll check his appointments," said Jorge. "Please, please, sit." He motioned to a leather couch up against the wall.

Melissa and Graeme sat. The heat of the tropics was drawing

sweat from her armpits, the backs of her knees, between her breasts. I need water, she thought, and a shower, and then baby powder. Lots of baby powder.

There was a single magazine on the coffee table, *Police Battle*, its cover showing a blurry Filipino man, his head too close to the camera, cradling either his ruined arm or a handful of barbecued chicken. Barney stood on the other side of the table swinging his arms, clapping his hands in front and then behind. Half moons of sweat spread out from under his armpits.

The building resonated with typewriter bells and ringing telephones. Melissa stretched out her legs and put her head back. We're on a sandy beach already, she thought, waiting for someone to bring our drinks. That was how the women at work described their vacations — one minute you're on the plane and the next you're drunk in your bathing suit.

It had been only three days since she'd worked her last shift at the Tie Rack in Pacific Centre Mall. It hadn't been a bad job, but she'd hated those last few minutes on the way in when the Skytrain went underground and everything outside the windows went black, when she would imagine that there had been a nuclear holocaust and that the human race had been forced beneath the surface. Those moments had convinced her that breathing the open air of the Philippines, even the deepest jungle air, would be a good idea.

"There is some confusion," said Jorge. "Most of the mission workers, you know, go directly to their stations. If they do come to the office, it is only to drop off paperwork. You are not here to drop off paperwork?"

"I don't think we were given any paperwork, were we?" she said.

"Nope," said Barney.

"You have met Mr. Thomas before, though, right? Most people don't come right to the head office. You're his friends."

"We've heard he's a … he's a great man," said Barney. "But —"

"Then why," asked Jorge, rising to his feet, "were you sent by your CWF chapter?"

"We were the only ones interested," Graeme said, a little too loudly.

"But you *were* approached with a posting. What was it? I have no record of anything. Do you know Mr. Duffy, is that what it is? Are you trying to find him?"

"The head office told the Vancouver office that there were missionary opportunities in the Philippines," said Melissa.

"They did?" asked Jorge. "Are you doctors?"

"Listen, we were *sent* for," said Barney. "This is supposed to be about Jesus Christ our saviour, not all this bullshit!"

"Excuse me, sir," said Jorge. "The fellowship is permitted to operate by the government of the Philippines only because we adhere to specific guidelines. The reason—"

"Will you just save it?" said Barney.

Melissa got up from the couch and crossed the foyer to the door. She went out and down the steps. The city smelled as though it were built inside a derelict refrigerator. She started up the sidewalk for the 7-Eleven. Segments of the pavement were missing, darkness running beneath them, so she moved into the middle of the street.

Little children raced out of their shacks and hurried in a knot after her, shouting, "Hello, missus! Whas your name?" They carried little bows strung with rubber bands and handfuls of drinking straws for arrows.

Teenaged boys with gold necklaces stood chewing gum in front of the 7-Eleven. The security guard held the door for her and her hip bumped against his revolver as she hurried into the air-conditioned interior. She stopped near a rack of chocolate bars and looked out at the children playing security-guard-with-gun, shooting each other with their fingers and falling down amid swells of laughter. A businessman with a double chin stood a few feet from her with an open magazine in his hands, giving Melissa a leisurely ogle. Her nipples were getting hard from the air conditioning so she folded her arms. She picked up a pack of cigarettes, Salems, from a large cardboard display and set them down on the counter.

"Forty," said the woman at the till. The security guard watched Melissa through the door. She pulled her T-shirt up a few inches and unzipped her money belt.

The guard held the door for her as she went out and as it whined shut behind her she pulled back the top of the pack and took out a cigarette. One of the teenaged boys cracked his gum and held up a lighter for her. It had a sticker on the side of a naked white woman holding her breasts up as if they were pieces of fruit. The boy pressed the lighter into her hand, a present, and she nodded a thank you, holding the smoke in for as long as she could. Then she let it out. She hadn't smoked since before they got married.

"Missionary?" asked the guard. He jerked his chin up the block, toward the CWF office.

Melissa took another puff and tried to fight back a cough. "I'm afraid so," she said.

She stuffed the pack into her pocket and started back, children racing around her, whooping now. They all seemed to have scabs on their knees and elbows and their noses ran in an inevitable yellow pour. One child shot at her with his finger and suddenly the rest followed his example, stringing their arrows and letting them fly into her legs and bottom as she walked away. She barely felt them. A wad of spit was welling in the back of her throat, so she dropped the cigarette on the sidewalk.

Barney was waiting on the steps with his hands in his pockets.

"What's up?" she asked. "What have you concocted for us?"

"I don't need that," he said. "I thought it would be easier." He lifted his shoe and studied the bottom of it. "He's finding out where we can go. We shouldn't have to jump through hoops. We just want to contribute."

She went back into the foyer, nearly banging the wooden door into her son. Jorge stood behind him with plastic transparencies and coloured markers in his hand.

"Okay. Everything is fine, actually," Jorge said. "They've agreed to let you go to Lintek and begin your good work there. There is a worker named Theodore Duffy who we sent there some time ago, a very excellent missionary. If you could join him, it would be quite helpful. Everyone here likes Mr. Duffy's work very much. We haven't had word from him in some time and there are concerns."

"Lintek," said Barney. "Got it."

"The fellowship has had a truck donated by our affiliates in West Virginia, so this afternoon we will give you a ride to the bus station."

"Can you tell Mr. Thomas we've been here?" asked Barney. "Tell him we're friends of Harry Egan."

"So," said Graeme, "we *are* going somewhere,"

Barney worked for the Parks Board for years, until he reached a supervisory position, and almost as soon as he did they cut the supervisory staff by half. He had seniority over everybody else, from the guys spreading fish fertilizer on up, but he'd signed a new contract with his promotion that didn't allow him to go back down the ladder — he either had a job or he didn't.

"Well, they told me when I got it," he said to Melissa, "that a guy who didn't smoke wouldn't last long." One of the few times he could joke about it.

He did his duty after that, going to the musty job-search room in the Sinclair Centre and toying with the margins on his résumé. He was unemployed for six months, then a year. It was the rainiest year in Vancouver history: 4500 millimetres.

Eventually he gave up the search and started sleeping in. He would stop in to see Melissa at Pacific Centre — her cute husband, the girls would tease her — and have coffee at the food fair with Bob Watson. He had been Barney's overseer at the Parks Board but had retired before the lay-off. Melissa found it hard not to be sarcastic about his toupée.

"I don't even know if I want to work again," Barney told Bob one day. Melissa was sitting with them on her break and she raised an eyebrow. "I don't like where I'm at, of course, but nothing else appeals to me."

"You have a Bible at home?"

"Yeah, I think so. Sure. Somebody gave one to Graeme."

"Try reading the Sermon on the Mount. Matthew 5. It's worth doing."

"If I get a chance."

Barney told Melissa that the Sermon on the Mount made a lot of sense, that every word of it was easy to agree with. According to Bob, the church group the Watsons belonged to stuck strictly to the Gospel. They weren't concerned with politics or sitting in judgement on people or preparing for the end of the world or any of that.

"The Bible has *focus*," Barney told her. "It's unbelievable." By the time he'd finished Acts in the New Testament, he realized that Jesus had stealthily come into him. He smiled at the cupboards in the kitchen and felt like he was on drugs again. He sat up in the middle of the night and explained it to Melissa because he was too excited to sleep.

When he got to the end of the Bible he went back and memorized his favourite parts. He led a discussion group on the first book of Samuel and talked about what it would take for a man to throw himself on his sword as Saul did. Then he wanted to concentrate on Jesus, so he carried a blue New Testament in his pocket.

A lot of the men in the congregation were there because the previous phases of their lives had ended: they'd come off drugs; they'd stopped drinking; they were freshly divorced; they'd lost their jobs. What families they had went along for the ride.

On Sunday mornings they all went to the Christian elementary school and Melissa and Graeme would do their best to join in the songs that Barney sometimes led in his quavering voice, standing up there in his striped polo shirt and cords. She marvelled at the contrast between this Barney and the one who had stood in a purple spotlight to the left of the drum set, shaking his long hair like a lunatic. Which one was more genuine? She repeated the prayers and if she had a sick friend she would say that person's name so the congregation could pray for them. She went through the motions without fail.

But Jesus was not in her heart or anywhere else in that vicinity. While Barney stood up and shouted and others stood up with him and shouted and Dr. Webster the dentist started speaking in tongues, she sat quietly on her creaking plastic chair. She imagined that belief was like one of those bizarre 3-D pictures that some people can walk up to and instantly see the shapes of a lioness and her cubs, but the next person could screw up their eyes and stamp their feet and never see anything but a blur.

They rode through the night in a jeepney — one of the silver buses decorated with decals and cattle horns and reflectors. There was a weak glow from an illuminated Jesus on the dashboard, but otherwise the only light was from the passengers' cigarettes.

Barney was asleep again, sitting close to the driver on the opposite bench, his knees up and his feet propped on a sack of rice. They'd tried to sit next to one another, but the Filipinos had darted between them as they'd clambered on, as though there was an unspoken plan to keep the three of them apart. Now they swayed with each pitch of the vehicle like a field of sleepy wheat.

Graeme sat opposite Melissa as well but farther to the rear, and only when he leaned forward into the dim light could she see his face. It was pinched with fatigue. Next to him sat an old woman without a tooth in her head who smoked cigarettes continuously. Now and then she would pat his knee, just to see how it felt, it seemed, so she could tell her old-women friends about it.

Melissa looked around at the other families dozing on the benches — little girls on their fathers' laps, a young couple asleep in matching *Titanic* T-shirts — but there was no way she could sleep short of stretching out on the floor, which was crowded with luggage and livestock. She was wide awake among the wrinkled faces and piles of fruit.

Barney's head had pitched forward onto his knees, folding him like a pocket-knife. In Nana Jordan's albums she'd seen a photo of him at fourteen. The picture had been taken with the rest of the family, aunts and uncles crowded into the sickly yellow living room and poor Barney in the background, wanting to die. He had hair combed down over his ears and wore a terrible dress shirt and bad sweater. It was clear from the way Barney expected Graeme to step unobstructed from infancy into adulthood that he had forgotten an awkward teen Barney had ever existed.

The Church of Awkward Teens, she thought, that would be a real hit if any of them would come out of their bedrooms. No praying, only fidgeting and uncomfortable silence. All denominations welcome.

Her eyes had been resting on the smoking old woman when suddenly she hopped up from the bench and came and squatted on the baskets in front of Melissa. She gave a little salute from the side of her temple with the stub of her cigarette.

"Missionary?" she asked, smiling.

Melissa nodded. "How did you know that?"

"You very clean." She gave Melissa's knee a stroke with the back of her hand. "These boys, they look for gold mining?" She pointed a thumb at Barney. "Money, money," she said. "Gold mining."

"All missionaries," said Melissa.

The old woman rose for a moment to rearrange her skirt. "Jehovah's Witness?"

Melissa almost laughed: imagine if their mission were to teach native people to worship in a church without windows and to refuse blood transfusions. Of course, if the natives had never heard of churches or blood transfusions, then neither would be that strange. "We're not Jehovah's Witnesses."

The old woman's shoulders drooped. She studied Melissa's face. "Seventh-Day Adventist?"

"Christian Workers Fellowship," Melissa said softly.

The woman stood up again and put a hand to her ear.

"Christian Workers Fellowship," Melissa said. She wanted to point to the logo, but wasn't wearing her polo shirt.

The woman waved her hand dismissively and went back to her bench.

Melissa tried to sleep. The air seeping in the windows was cold now, but her jacket was inside the suitcase on top of the jeepney, so she wrapped her arms around herself. This is when you need a husband, she thought, a nice warm husband.

Jesus flickered off. The driver needed the cigarette lighter.

The night of the hot tub incident Barney lay wide awake until morning, wondering what the future could possibly hold for a kid like Graeme, who had no backbone and who would happily be moulded by the worst influences around him. The panhandling kids on Granville Street, studded leather jackets, green hair, cold sores. He told Melissa that was all he saw ahead for Graeme.

In the morning they let Graeme go over to Ernie's to watch movies — Ernie's parents were realtors and very trustworthy. Melissa scraped breakfast plates into the garbage while Barney sat at the table with the eternal classifieds in front of him.

"The one option we have is the military. Not like he has to be sent overseas or something, but a cadet troupe, something to walk him through this and out the other side."

"Walk him through what?" she asked.

"The bad patch."

"He's not so broken he has to be sent off for repairs."

Barney phoned Bob Watson, who suggested a Bible camp for the whole family — a week, two weeks. There was one in the Fraser Valley. Barney asked Melissa if she could get time off from the Tie Rack for that. Graeme came home in time for dinner. He'd been watching war movies. That was all he had to say to them.

The next morning Harry Egan talked to the congregation about what had drawn him into missionary work. First, he said with a shy smile, there had been a lot of ads on TV back then for the Peace Corps. "They said, 'When you tell them how you made a difference, people will say over and over again "I wish I'd done that."'" Isn't that great? Now, that got me thinking about what a huge world it was out there and what a lot of problems it had: disease, war, famine. Thirty years ago they had all the same problems we have today. Sure they did. For some reason, though, it never crossed my mind that there might still be missionaries working in the world. I thought they'd all finished what they were doing in darkest Africa and gone home in 1900. But one day I saw a poster on the train platform that said 'Trust in God — and do something.' What was that poster for? It was for CWF missionary work. Yes it was. I realized then and there that just as there were disease, war and famine there was Godlessness too, and that had to be the worst problem of all. Because even if the Peace Corps could go out and dig a well or feed some starving babies, in short, *save some lives*, that was nothing compared to what a man could do *saving souls*. Because whether people died now or died later, they would all have to walk up to God and be judged, wouldn't they? Now the fellowship had just been founded there in Chicago, so I shined up my best shoes and went down to the office. I was halfway through my business degree and my parents, my fiancée, none of them wanted me to go, but I went anyway. Do you know why?"

"Why?" asked Bob Watson.

"Because there is no time like the present to grab God in both fists."

Barney stood up and all heads turned to watch him.

"Harry," he said, "my family and I are ready to go. Graeme, Melissa." They stood up too, looking stunned. "We're ready to do the good work. We're ready to go out and do it."

And Harry Egan strode down the aisle and put his hands on Barney's shoulders. Everyone started clapping and whistling and Dr. Webster spoke in tongues. "For God's sake get to them first," Harry said. "Once they've got MTV they won't look at you."

Melissa felt sick to her stomach, even more so as the wives gathered around her, all of them patting her elbow and cooing over the courageous decision she'd made. They talked about fundraisers to pay for the airfare. Someone's daughter could look after the Jordans' house.

I'm not going, Melissa thought. I don't even know where it is, but I'm not going.

But afterward Barney took her hand and they walked out to the parking lot — the first time they'd held hands since Graeme was in elementary school — and for once Graeme walked alongside them instead of twenty feet behind. He hadn't realized yet that they really expected him to go. Barney had his shoulders back and his chin up, like that guy in high school who knew how to have a pretty good time.

If she didn't go, the marriage would be over, she knew that, and she knew that Harry's fiancée hadn't wanted him to go to the Amazon either and now they'd been married twenty-five years. So they would preach the Gospel and it would go badly or go well and the marriage would follow suit.

T W O

The jeepney stopped in Baguio and they piled out under a smoky sky. The air was cool; Melissa felt like putting on her grey cardigan until she remembered that it was in Canada. Vendors with bandanas around their heads and wispy beards stood around selling peanuts.

Barney waited beside the jeepney for the bags to be passed down, giving a smile and nod to every person in the crowd. His white pants were smudged with grease and his hands were on his hips like a quarterback on the sidelines.

"How are you? Nice to see you."

All the grandmothers and men in sunglasses gave him sideways looks.

When his bag came down, Graeme rummaged through it for

his green camouflage jacket. Over his dress shirt it looked more ridiculous than ever, but a teenaged Filipino boy in an identical jacket came over to him, bobbing his head in acknowledgement, as though he and Graeme were the first of the gang members to show up for the meeting.

"How are ya?" said Graeme.

"My friend," said the Filipino boy. "You want a tour? Rice terraces? Cliff graves? Rent a car?"

Now the men on the roof of the bus passed down Melissa's bag and she struggled to set it down beside Graeme's.

The Filipino boy looked her up and down, then at Graeme again.

"Missionaries," he said. "I pity you, my friend."

The sun found a peephole through the clouds and beat down on them as though through a magnifying glass.

"Who here's a missionary?" called out a big man, an African-American. "I've got to get my people picked up." He spotted the Jordans and came through the crowd, head and shoulders and baseball cap above everyone, and rested his hand on the Filipino boy's camouflaged shoulder. He put the other hand out to Melissa.

"I'm John Salk," he said. "How do you do?" He wore a T-shirt that said *Batting for God's Team.*

"I'm fine," said Melissa. His hand was cool and dry. "Feeling a bit knocked around."

"It's a long ride," John said. "I've been trying to get a truck, but you know how it is, everybody running around one way or the other. Once we're out in the villages, we'll be glad we don't have one, though. You just walk everywhere and you sleep on mats folks roll out for you. I'm working out of Tinapa right now and the river there is beautiful. Oh, hell, I'm sorry." He gave the Filipino boy a friendly pat that rocked his slender body. "Felix, were they with you? Am I stepping on your toes?"

159

Felix looked at the ground and grinned. "No, Mr. John."

"All right."

"I'm Barney Jordan," said Barney.

Melissa had forgotten about him. He stood with a heavy suit-case in each hand and somehow managed to look pleased with the entire situation. She'd expected him to be giving John Salk the who-the-hell-are-you look.

"This is my son, Graeme," said Barney. "You've met Melissa, my wife." He set down a suitcase and put out his hand. More teenagers were gathering behind him, most with their T-shirts pulled above their bellies. A few waved their hands over their heads and pointed at Melissa.

"You're with CWF?" asked Barney.

"CWF?" asked John. He glanced down at Felix with amusement. "I don't know what that is."

"It's the Christian Workers Fellowship."

"I've never heard of them. I'm more of a free agent, if you get my meaning."

"Nondenominational," said Graeme. He zipped up his jacket to hide the shirt underneath.

"That's right, son," said John. "That's right."

"So where are you talking about taking us, John?" asked Melissa. "We have to get to Lintek."

"Is that where you're heading? That's a long ways, up past the mining camps. I've never been there. Is that where that movie set is?"

"What movie?" asked Graeme.

"I just came back down, you know. It's funny, I had this feeling I had to get to Baguio and here you all are."

"What, did CWF get in touch with you?" said Barney. "Because we heard this guy was—"

"No, no, my friend," said John, and though he was looking at

Barney his hand reached out and touched Melissa on the arm. "I just knew you all would be here. Maybe that's God working, I don't know. I just get a feeling sometimes and this is what comes of it."

"I get the same feeling," said Barney.

"And nothing comes of it," said Melissa.

"Lucky for us, that's what I say," said Graeme. "Who knows what else we would've done."

"Make your own way," John asked, "is that how your people operate?"

"That's it," said Barney. "Like Indiana Jones."

"Hell, let's get a cold drink before we go anywhere else." John was already pushing through the crowd and they had to scramble for their bags to follow him. The back of his shirt said *Hittin' Them out of the Park*.

When they got to the main street, choked with traffic, John was waiting with his hat pushed back on his head. He rested one hand on his hip and the other stroked his beard.

"Now to get to Tinapa we're going to spend another day on a bus and those suitcases are a problem. There's a big place here sells army surplus, we can switch you over to duffel bags. Something more comfortable."

"Could we pick up the suitcases on our way back?" asked Barney.

Melissa couldn't believe he was being so agreeable to every suggestion.

John turned and surveyed the buildings around them: fruit stands, TV sales, boarded windows. He pulled his hat down and then pushed it up again. "Cordillera Hotel has lockers," he said. "All right. Mount up."

They dragged their suitcases, scraping them along the pavement, grinding down their plastic corners. The noise acted

like a public address system: *We're not from here! We're idiots!*
Grim-faced men with briefcases stepped out of their way. Barney
gave Melissa and Graeme a jokey smile.

"Once you lose the suitcases," John said over his shoulder,
"it'll be a turning point."

It was late afternoon. John smoked a cigarette, carrying a gym
bag in one hand and the contents of Melissa's toilet kit in a net
bag over his shoulder.

"Car coming," he said.

They all stepped into the long grass, except Graeme, who
stayed where he was, looking up the road.

"Graeme, let's go," said Barney.

A pick-up truck loaded with people rounded the corner, five
or six men hanging off each side, and the driver leaned on the
horn. The men on the side shouted and each threw up a free
hand like a police officer saying stop, as though Graeme were
hurtling toward *them*. He took one step, all he had time for, but
stayed in the path of the bumper festooned with Filipino flags
and STP stickers. John stepped toward him, picked him up under
the armpit and they both fell back into the brush.

The truck screamed past and John got to his feet, pulling a
twig off the back of his pants. He picked up the string bag.

"Everybody all right?"

The road was conspicuously empty now. Green hillsides rose
up around them. No one answered. Barney shook his head.

"Oh my God," said Melissa.

"That was dangerous," said John. "I don't know *how* that got
to be so dangerous, but that was dangerous."

"Graeme, get up now," said Melissa.

"'The ways of the Lord are right,'" said Barney. "'The righteous walk in them, but the rebellious stumble.' Hosea 14:9."

"Part of doing this," said Graeme, "was to *experience* things for ourselves. That's what I thought."

"But the first rule for missionaries," said John, "is to never let them see you get killed."

It was twilight when they reached Tinapa. They crossed a wooden bridge over a muddy yellow river and came into the village. A spire towered above the rooftops and when they drew nearer they saw that the church was painted a dull pink and adorned with climbing roses.

Three dogs trotted out to give the new arrivals a cursory sniff. John led the Jordans up the street. It was meal time. A few villagers relaxed at tables outside their doors. *"Magandang gabi,"* they said, raising hands in greeting as the party passed. The men all wore singlet undershirts — like Marlon Brando, Melissa thought, in that movie where he was always yelling.

"Magandang gabi po," John called back.

"It's a lovely place," said Melissa.

"It's base camp," said John. "From here on it's five or six days up into the hills. Each day strips away a bit more of what we'd call civilization and every day you feel it stronger — you're meant to be up there."

"Smell the air," said Barney.

There was a mountain cleanness to it, along with the tang of animal droppings and marijuana.

They came to a small house at the top of the street. John led them across its dusty porch, where a cat lay asleep on a table, and pushed past a blanket hung across the doorway. The marijuana smell was strong. Melissa's shoulder ached from the strap of the duffel bag but the room was too dark to see where to put it down. She heard a chicken clucking and she could make out the ember of a cigarette in the corner. It was so reminiscent of the jeepney that she wondered if all the other passengers were in here too — she'd been in the Philippines for such a short time that every new thing reminded her of the previous thing.

"Angie, for the love of Pete, turn some lights on," said John. "Where's the gas lamp?"

"I've got it," said a woman's voice. "Wait, it's over here." The lamp flared up to reveal a girl shorter than Melissa, with blonde-and-red dreadlocks. She wore ragged green shorts and a patterned blouse, probably woven in the village. Her joint smouldered in a glass ashtray on the floor. She was Canadian — a big maple leaf adorned the backpack leaning against the hearth. Two silvery-headed chickens came out from under the kitchen table. Angie stood there blinking. The smell of chickens was strong.

"John, man, you're back already?"

"I always come back," he said. "I'm the cat who came back. Say, aren't you all from Canada too? Is that what you said?"

"Vancouver," said Melissa. She dropped her bag.

"I'm from Winnipeg!" said Angie. "That's cool. I haven't seen a Canadian since, oh boy, I don't know, Mindanao. Where are *you* from, John? Was it Nebraska?" She set the lamp down on the table as the chickens strutted over to Barney and scowled at his leg.

"Ohio," murmured John. He waded over to a double bed in the corner. It was buried under bundles of mildewed newspapers and boxes of video cassettes, and he threw everything onto the floor with a bang. One of the chickens gave a flap of warning.

"Hey, D.O.A. is from Vancouver!" said Angie. "I've seen them live, three times."

"I was in a band in Vancouver," said Barney. "Long time ago."

"Get out of here, which one?"

"The Fairbridge Brothers Blues Band."

That was the name, thought Melissa. Her father had met the Fairbridge brothers once at the apartment and referred to them forever after as the Kings of the Dopeheads.

"Huh," said Angie.

"You sang rock and roll and now you sing in the choir?" asked John.

"He wasn't the singer," said Graeme. "He played the bass."

"Oh, the workhorse," said John. "Man's got to work to get noticed."

"Hey," Graeme said to Angie. "I'm Graeme."

Angie stuck her joint in the side of her mouth to shake hands with him.

To Melissa that gesture too was reminiscent of their band days — that was how they'd gone around meeting each other.

Angie picked up her ashtray. "Are you guys just travelling around, or are you in on the Jesus thing with this guy?"

"The Jesus thing," said Barney. "Definitely the Jesus thing."

"Angie and I met up the valley a ways," said John. He was sweeping feathers off the bed. "I'm slowly trying to bring her around."

"Very slowly," said Angie.

"I guess I'm thinking if I can crack her then I can drum God into anybody. Here now." He unfolded a clean sheet and snapped it in the air so it settled onto the mattress, air gusting beneath the fabric. Melissa felt exhaustion waft over her. "You folks take a seat right here," said John. "I'll get these out of your way." He stacked the boxes of videotapes in the corner.

"What's all that for?" asked Barney.

John grinned. "Movie night. Fella down the road's got a VCR, so I show them *Rebel Without a Cause*, *Seven Samurai*, *Once Upon a Time in the West*, all classics. Anything with a martyr in it's good for getting the message across. They're Baptists here anyway, but what the heck, we have a good time. Listen, I'm going to throw together something to eat. Angie, you want to pass that thing around?"

"It's nearly done," Angie said. She had settled back on her cushion. "And I thought they were all religious and that."

John took the joint. "This is the old-time religion," he said.

"Think I'll get some air," said Barney.

Melissa followed him out. Graeme unbuttoned his dress shirt as Melissa walked past.

It was dark now on the porch, just a few minutes past sundown. Barney leaned against the table and the cat stood up and meowed.

"Sorry, young fella," he said. He stroked the cat's head.

"What do you think of all this?" Melissa asked.

Barney studied her for a while. The cat purred. "I don't know," he said. "It seems like it might be the best way to do things. Things we want to do. I don't know what I imagined." He pulled the cat onto his lap. "What did you imagine?"

"There's nothing wrong with this."

They stood and listened to sounds inside the room, Angie's peal of laughter. The hillsides were full of frogs, grating and hiccuping. Barney put his hand out and drew her closer. After the months, years, of limbo, here they finally were: a terrific couple fixed on adventure, to be looked upon and admired. This was a great moment in their marriage.

"I love you," she said, too quickly.

The cat pulled its shoulders back and stretched its front legs. Barney rubbed it under the chin. "Love you too," he said.

Melissa shifted her weight. They could hear men shouting on the road.

"Well, what do you think of *her*?" she asked.

"I don't think we'll be spending a lot of time together."

They went back in. Graeme had taken his shirt off and put

the camouflage jacket back on over his hairless chest. He was leaning forward against his knees, looking at Angie. She was staring at the ashtray.

"This water's never going to boil," said John. "I'm just going to go ahead and throw these things in, you take a seat. Listen, how much Tagalog do you all know? Not that that's what most of them speak, but it's a start. Or Ilocano. Do you know any of that?"

"Well," said Barney. "We ..."

"Don't you have a phrase book?" asked John. "Angie, don't you have one?"

"Fell apart."

Melissa lay back on the bed, her feet still on the floor. Moths circled above her. She closed her eyes.

"*Magandang gabi*, Mr. John!" A man in a tie and white shirt peered in past the blanket. He wore a couple of gold chains over his shirt.

"Arnoldo, my brother. Come on in," said John, wiping his hands. "Bible study — is it Thursday? *Huwebes*?"

"*Opo, Huwebes*," said Arnoldo, and he sauntered in, a thick Bible under his arm. Another dozen or so people followed him, men and women dressed in their finery, carrying more Bibles and taking seats where they could find them. Angie and Graeme moved into the corner. A young couple with a baby sat down next to Melissa, their clothes laden with odd smells.

"Okay," said John, clapping his hands. "Can you stab those spuds in a minute? *Tuloy! Kumusta ka?* What are we on, Sylvia, Luke 4?"

Graeme and Angie were going to sleep next to each other on rattan mats. He sat with his blanket over his legs and took his jacket off, then rummaged through his bag, taking out his comb, his toothbrush, putting them back in, taking them back out. Angie lay on her side looking up at him. Watching from the bed, Melissa was surprised to see how well muscled his torso was. After a minute Angie rolled over with her back to him and he slumped down onto his mat. He pulled the blanket over his white shoulder.

Melissa leaned over and turned off the lamp. For a few minutes Barney read Ephesians with his penlight.

She stayed awake, especially once the penlight was off and Barney began to snore. She wondered if she was only capable of sleeping in Canada and, if so, how long she could survive in the Philippines. A couple of weeks? Eventually she might fall into a luxurious coma.

She remembered she had cigarettes and set her foot on the floor. There was a cluck of surprise.

John lay in a hammock across the porch. She assumed he was asleep since he didn't say a word as she stood in the doorway and lit up, but after a moment his hand reached over to push against the table and start the hammock rocking. Bugs flew past the porch, clicking amiably.

"Can I ask you something, John?" she said quietly.

"You don't have to call me John." His voice sounded like his chin was against his chest.

"What would you prefer I call you?"

"You don't have to call me anything."

The first few drags made her dizzy. The wooden door frame was soft against her shoulder, as though countless women before her had leaned in the same spot.

"Do you have a wife?"

"Heh." He exhaled a little laugh. "That's what everybody wants to know. Well."

There was a long pause, filled with her slow smoking and his slow rocking. She wondered what awful information he could have to convey that required so much thought. A dog yowled. The cigarette was nearly finished.

"There was a girl I knew from back home, a friend of the family, and everyone sort of decided we were sweet on each other. But I joined the army instead. Thought it was a good way to get into college one day. I never went to college, of course. Can you imagine? No, I'm happy out here."

She tried lighting a new cigarette off the old one, muttering *mm-hm*.

"It's all peaceful now, this kind of night. But they used to say there were guerrillas in the jungle here, you know, Communist guerrillas. This was twenty years ago, when I first came up here. Marcos implemented martial law, supposedly so they could control those Communists, but that was just so they all could get rich. They tortured innocent people all over the country."

She sat on the edge of the railing. She could see him clearly, in his T-shirt, with one arm flopped over his head.

"You weren't scared?"

"Hm. One of the Episcopalians, guy from Arizona, he disappeared, but they didn't seem to want me. They wouldn't take the head of a village either, but they'd take the guy who made shoes. Just a roll of the dice. They said this one shoemaker was conspiring against the army, so they cut off his arm and dumped him back in front of his house. That was over in Apayao. I was starting a school there. It was the middle of the night and his relatives came to get me because the shoemaker said he wanted to hear about the baby Jesus. He just wanted to hear *something*. I didn't have much of the language so I read it in English. He couldn't have heard me anyway, he was so messed up. One time, you know, I saw a cat get hit by a car and this guy was like that, panting and writhing, knowing he wasn't going to make it. They tried to tie a belt around his armpit like a tourniquet, but there was nothing left of his shoulder. Belt kept falling off."

"And *that* didn't scare you?"

"I have to tell you, I saw God that night. I looked at all the people around his bed, praying, trying to take care of him, crying while he stared up at them, and it was like there was a light over each of their heads. Those people were strong. God was testing the Philippines back then, you know, like he tested Vietnam and Russia and Poland and blacks in America and all the rest. Like he tested Israel in Exodus and Samuel. What is that, a Marlboro Light?"

"Salem."

"Really? Oh, you've been down in Manila, that's right. Can I ask you for one?"

"Sure." Melissa passed it to him over the webbing of the hammock.

He grabbed her index finger first, then found the cigarette.

"What about the woman?" she asked.

He smiled at her in the dark. She could almost hear his cheeks crinkling.

"Of course. Irene. We never got to that. Well, I was at Clark Air Force Base north of Manila all the years the war was on in Vietnam. Six times I applied to do a tour, but the officers never let me. I was looking after their paperwork, so they made it so I never budged. Oh, don't get me wrong, they did me a favour — otherwise I'd be talking to you out of a body bag. Anyhow, Irene got married to a plumber. Stayed married twenty years, had a couple of kids, but then they separated and she started writing letters again. I think she thought this whole thing, out in the jungle, handing out penicillin, burping babies, she thought that was all pretty sexy — can I say that in front of a lady?"

"By all means."

"Anyhow, she didn't want to come out to the Philippines because she'd heard that it was dirty and that the shopping wasn't good. She said instead we could meet in Singapore. There's a lot of malls in Singapore."

"Did you go?"

"Oh, yeah. We got adjoining rooms at the hotel. I've still got some pay from the government, so I could afford it. But the whole thing was no good. We rode around on the subway, you know, it looks out over the buildings where people hang their washing — I liked that. But otherwise it was no good. I told her she could send her kids out here to the Philippines for a look around if they wanted, but she said *never*. What's there to be scared of? I don't know."

Melissa sat there for a long moment, leaning on the railing. She lobbed her cigarette butt into the road and it sparked on the gravel.

"Maybe when she saw you in person you were more sexy than she could stand."

"That's probably it, that's right. That's probably what it was." He gave himself another push off the table. "But it's funny, cause I had high hopes for Irene. I knew some women over here over the years, but that wasn't the same. They're not from where I'm from."

Melissa stood up. "I'm ready to climb into bed."

"With the husband. That's all right. You're putting on a good show."

"What?"

"I mean, what's it called? Happy Christian Fellows?" He folded his hands over his chest. "I don't think you're it. Maybe I'm wrong, but I think you're here for show. Show what a happy family looks like. The family martyr. Something along those lines."

"Um, okay," she said. "Good night."

One evening in Vancouver, Melissa came home from work and found Barney asleep in the bath tub. It was June, still bright outside, with swallows whizzing past the windows. Graeme was at a friend's. Barney's head lay back among the shampoo bottles, a magazine called *Testament* half on the side of the tub and half in the water, his genitals floating weightlessly on the surface. His feet looked bony, tucked under the taps. It could have been a crime movie, his body a prop for the autopsy scene.

She sat on the lid of the toilet and his eyelids flickered. "Shoot," he said, and held the sodden magazine over the water. She undid the straps on her shoes and slid them off onto the bathmat.

"Mrs. Jordan," he finally said. "How was your day?"

"The same. Was your day any different from the day before?"

He squinted at her, as if he needed glasses. She took off her earrings and put them beside the sink.

"You got something in mind for dinner?" he asked.

She untucked her white blouse, undid the top button and pulled it off over her head. She dropped it on her shoes.

"Here's a quiz," she said.

"What about?"

"First kisses."

"I remember those." He moved the magazine so that it would drip onto the bathmat. The water went all over her blouse.

She slid her bra off her shoulders and rose to her feet.

"Tell me about the first one."

"The ramp by the cafeteria."

"What else?"

"It was ... it was in the morning."

"It was after lunch. Right afterward I went to sewing class. Who instigated the kiss?" She dropped her skirt onto the pile and started to roll down the top of her pantyhose.

"It was mutual."

"I kissed you, because you'd only wanted to *hug*. Do you remember why that was?"

"No."

172

"You saw an episode of *Happy Days* where Richie finds out that if you play innocent and hug a girl she'll wind up kissing you. So you tried it. That's what you told me."

"I was clever."

"I guess so."

She pulled her underwear off her ankle.

"Here, I'll get out."

"Stay in."

She'd imagined that, despite everything, they were still coming from the same place, the same beginning, that they were tethered to it like a pair of kites. But the older their son got and the more he made his own choices, the more Melissa was away from home, the less interest Barney had in the family. As far as he was concerned the experiment was over.

She lay down with him in the cold water.

There was a smell blowing down the valley of something rotting. Terraced rice fields crept up the slope. Melissa watched John's sandals as they padded along the road.

"You been out here before?" Graeme asked.

"Oh, yeah," Angie said. Her backpack was as big as she was. "There are graves on the cliffs up there. Bones lying around. People here figure the living shouldn't forget about the dead, so they keep them where they can see them, you know?"

"That's like Jesus," said Graeme, furrowing his brow. "He's dead, but we don't forget about him."

"Well said," said Barney. "Full points."

"I guess so," said Angie. "I think every religion starts from the same point."

"What's that?" asked Graeme.

"Everybody dies," said Angie. "And religions get invented to deal with that. And in Christianity the rest of the rules deal with the fact that everybody likes fucking."

"Angie!" said John.

"Just getting a rise out of ya."

The roar of an engine passed behind a thicket and just ahead Melissa could see where their road merged with another. On the corner was a shack with signs for Coca-Cola and Benson & Hedges. Strings of candy hung in the window.

"Keep your eyes peeled for a dump truck or something," said John. "Something big. Guys from the mining company will take you most of the way to where you're going. After that you'll have to walk. Lintek is up the river a ways. I haven't been all the way, but I heard there are still indigenous tribes up there. Sounds like your thing, doesn't it? Animism, you know. Channelling ancestors. They've probably got it all."

"Aren't you coming with us, John?" asked Graeme. "Angie, aren't you going to come?"

"Well, yeah, it sounds cool," said Angie. She looked at Barney. "No tour groups up there, right?"

"Fine with me," said Barney. "Do as you like."

"You just go and get it done," said John, "and we'll hook up when you come back down. Let's go a little farther, the trucks can't pull in here."

"You've got things to do yourself," said Barney.

"Well, for one thing, I've got movie night!" said John. "*Rocky* at seven o'clock. Just the first one, mind you. Once he starts winning, it does me no good."

"But you need to tell us," said Melissa, "what to expect."

Their driver was heavyset and wore a khaki fishing vest and a baseball cap with military insignia on the beak. They'd been coughing out thank-yous since they'd wedged themselves into the cab, but after several hours he'd still not said a word in reply. Now it had rained torrentially for twenty minutes and stopped just as abruptly. The truck was stuck up to its axles in mud.

A gang of Filipina women came through the brush beside the road, sacks of rice and stacked flats of San Miguel beer on their backs, held by taut straps across their foreheads. The driver slid from his seat to the ground and held an American five-dollar bill above the women's heads.

Melissa sat crammed behind the driver's seat. She watched in the side mirror as the women squatted beside the road to let their loads down, then straightened up and disappeared behind the truck. She could see part of one woman with her shoulder against the tailgate. The women were going to push them out of the mud.

The driver climbed back in and smiled at Barney. He gunned the engine, let the emergency brake go and released the clutch. For a second they sat immobile, then lurched up onto the harder ground, the driver working the wheel. In the mirror Melissa watched the women tumble forward like bowling pins. The driver shifted into second, then triumphantly turned his hand over to display his five-dollar bill. Angie gave a snort of disgust. The trees and hillsides rattled by.

"But you don't have any Bibles?" asked Carl. He was the mine's assistant foreman. "You're missionaries, but you don't have Bibles?"

"We're just getting a feel for it," said Barney.

"And what's that name of the place you want to get to?"

"Lintek."

"Here, wait a second. Joe! Joe, come over here!"

Machinery roared just over the hill. One of the workers with a kerchief over his face came trotting over, swinging his shovel. The other men stopped working. Iron buckets from digging machines lay discarded here and there like dice.

Joe pulled down his kerchief. His eyes and forehead were filthy black; his nose and lips were clean. "Nothing here," he said. He pointed up into the trees. "Maybe there."

"Listen, Lintek, you know it? Is that around here?"

"Lintek very famous. Make the movie there."

"What movie?" asked Carl. "What are you talking about?"

"Is it *Apocalypse Now*?" asked Graeme.

"Don't you know Lintek?" asked Joe.

"No, of course I don't!" said Carl. "That's what I'm asking you!"

"How do we get there?" asked Melissa.

Joe pointed up into the trees again. They all had to shade their eyes. Birds circled over the forest.

"Keep walking up." Joe made an incline with his hand. "Sometimes you hear *bang!* That is Lintek."

"It goes bang?" asked Carl.

Joe nodded and pulled the kerchief back up over his mouth.

"I thought we could follow a river," said Melissa.

"That used to be the case," said Carl. "See, we had to divert that about a mile. Do you want to take a look?"

The other workers watched Joe coming and cut in with their shovels.

"Oh, we don't have a whole lot of time," Barney said.

"Sorry, yeah. I think everybody who comes up here's an investor, but that's not you guys, is it? Lot of investment opportunity here, though, maybe you want to take some literature with you?"

"I'll take something," said Angie. "You got a pamphlet?"

They slept under a tarp, next to the river. It was shallow and clear here; the mud that flowed past Tinapa had started from the gold mine. Now they'd moved beyond that kind of progress.

All afternoon Angie cut creepers with her machete and passed them down the line for the Jordans to suck water from. That was all they had to eat or drink; Barney had thought their supply of peanuts would last longer than it had. Angie stopped talking to Graeme about smoking up or ska bands she'd seen in San Diego. Barney was quiet. He had no scripture relevant to crawling through tropical forest. The Bible takes place in the desert.

It rained in the night and it made a peaceful sound on the tarp. Melissa imagined all the animals that were out there crowding under the tarp with them, the mongoose saying *What a great idea* to the wild pig.

The river murmured close by. They lay on their duffel bags and as he fell asleep Barney rolled against Melissa and snuggled his head under her chin. His hand lay insubstantial on her stomach. She wondered why she felt so critical of him now, when for years she'd been so good at treasuring some part of him — some promise in him — and ignoring the rest. Maybe it was his moustache. There'd been no moustache when she'd fallen in love with him. Missionaries weren't supposed to have moustaches, just race car drivers and policemen. Missionaries could have *beards*, but there was never anything in the Bible about Abraham and his terrific moustache, waxed and twirled as scripture commanded. She pictured a bunch of prophets dressed like the Great Gatsby, leaning against their Studebakers. She let sleep take over.

Then she could hear Angie whispering on the other side of Barney. Melissa raised her head the slightest bit to see over her husband and there was Angie, overlapping Graeme. They were kissing. Melissa put her head down again. Her heart was pounding. Right next to his parents? Maybe in the Philippines, up here in the hills, that's how it's done. There weren't any drive-ins.

She counted to fifty before looking again. It was only for a second and then she dropped her head down. Graeme's penis was in Angie's hand.

Melissa's heart was beating in her ears and the sound of the rain was miles away. But she heard something overtop of it.

Did a light move across the tarp? Barney slept on. She lifted her head. Angie was on one elbow now beside Graeme, head up and listening too — his thing had been put away. Was it a voice? The river was loud, malevolent.

A flashlight shone in her face, then off, onto the others, not long enough for her vision to come back. Barney sat up and a brown hand came out of the blackness to push him down. No one said anything. Three flashlights, now four. She went up on her elbows. The flashlight shone in her eyes.

"Dasaho opedeka."

"Iha damuti mangopa-gopa."

Barney sat up again and a pair of hands grabbed him violently by the shirt.

"Aiee!"

The hands released him, retreating out of the light. Barney stayed rigid, ready, no doubt, for the spear that would run him through. Then the hands reappeared, moving slowly. They gently patted Barney's chest this time, smoothing out his shirt. A thumb moved lovingly over the CWF logo.

An old man, the owner of the hands, kneeled down in the light and Melissa blinked several times to focus on him. He was shirtless, leathery and brown, with feathers tied around one arm and a black *Star Wars: Episode I* baseball cap perched high on his head. He smelled of wood smoke.

"*Larahnangow*," he whispered to her. His hand snaked out to pinch the side of her neck and she tried to twist away, but already his hand was pulling back. He held a thick black leech. Blood coursed down his arm.

"You know Mr. Ted Duffy?" he asked.

T H R E E

I t was a long way to Lintek through the dark and the mud and more than once Melissa slid back down to the bottom of the path, knocking down Graeme or whoever was behind her. "How do you say sorry?" she yelled. Every few feet they passed a waterfall.

"They don't speak Tagalog," said Angie. "It's some dialect."

"We speak *English*," said the old man. "My name, Kilgore."

"Like in the movie?" asked Graeme.

Melissa could barely make out the whiteness of his face.

Every few minutes men would disappear to the left or right with their feathers and spears, reappearing a minute later from the opposite side. A warrior with a necklace of teeth bent a branch back for them. They couldn't be human teeth, Melissa consoled herself, unless the person had been so bucktoothed as to be deformed.

"How'd you learn English?" asked Angie.

"Mr. Duffy," said Kilgore. "But Manong named me Kilgore. He change everybody's name. Everybody scared of Manong, so they say okay. His name Lance," he said, and pointed to the man with the necklace.

179

Lance gave a hang-ten sign.

"Where'd he learn that?" asked Angie.

"Manong teach him."

Graeme sunk to his knee in mud and Barney put his arms around him as he pulled his leg up again. It made a sound like water sucked down a drain.

"Well, Dad," shouted Graeme.

"I know," said Barney.

The flashlight beams played in all directions, lighting up the rain like shards of glass.

By daylight they came to the end of the valley. The river still threaded through the woods beside them.

They stopped where a tree had fallen across the path and one of the men gripped the trunk to pull it aside, glancing at his comrades. Lance and Kilgore studied the treetops. Melissa gave Barney a questioning look and he shrugged.

The man pulled back the tree and the rest of them screamed — a head sat on a spike in the middle of the path. The features looked Chinese, the skin mouldy. The muscles jerked in Melissa's arms and the tiny hairs stood on end. The men started to laugh.

"It from movie!" said Kilgore. "*Nay pah moaning!* We all very scared!"

"*Aiee!*" said Lance.

Barney knocked on the forehead; it was made of fibreglass. "Graeme, this is from a movie?" he asked.

"*Apocalypse Now,*" said Graeme. "With Martin Sheen. You guys saw it, right? In your pre-, uh, pre-Christian phase."

"Yeah, we *did*," said Melissa. "With Linda and Brad, remember?"

They shouldered their bags and continued walking.

"Ernie and I were *so* into it," said Graeme. "He's got the wide screen. The head must be from the part where they come to the compound, right, and his enemies are strung up on poles or their heads are on the wall. It's sort of in the background when you're watching, 'cause you're worried about Willard. But they're Kurtz's enemies."

"Kurtz!" Lance whispered.

The men stopped in their tracks. Kilgore turned to Barney.

"Manong is the prophet of Kurtz. He waits for Kurtz to come back and we wait too. Sometimes Willard comes instead. Mr. Ted Duffy was Willard."

"Now *you* are Willard," said Lance.

"You are all Willard," said Kilgore. He motioned them up the trail. The forest around them was silent.

"If Mr. Duffy's your buddy," Angie whispered over her shoulder, "isn't he supposed to be yelling at them about Jesus?"

"We don't yell about Jesus," said Barney. "We get a feel for the community and its needs."

"That head," Graeme asked, "is that all that's left of the set? I mean, where did they actually film the movie?"

"They make movie *here*," said Kilgore, pointing at the ground. "*Nay pah moaning.* Do-do-do-do-do-do. Helicopter come." He circled his finger through the air. "Many people." He stopped short at the base of a tree.

Melissa could make out a skinny man far up in the branches, shirtless and deeply tanned, wearing cut-off jeans. His hands were clasped in prayer.

"Mr. Duffy!" yelled Kilgore. "We got Willard!"

"What's that?" asked Duffy. He had a British accent. He peered down at them through the leaves. "I'll come down." He slithered down the trunk, slipping from one branch to the next, and in a moment was on the ground.

"Hello, everyone." He put out a hand to Melissa, who was nearest to him. "Good Lord, visitors. And so many, what is it, four? I'm Theodore Duffy. Ted." He wore the same necklace as Lance, only the teeth looked human.

"We're with — he, my husband, is with CWF."

"What? Why, I can't believe it. Honestly? They sent you up here after me?"

"They said, 'Go to Lintek,'" said Graeme. "'He'll be there.'"

"Why, it's unbelievable! And where are you from?"

"Canada," said Angie.

"Why were you in the tree?" Barney asked.

"Oh, for my invocations. You know, it's a powerful substance, wood. Possesses energy we can never hope to understand."

Barney sighed. His shoulders were hunched under his load, his whole body stinking and streaked with grime. He was exhausted and pale, his eyes red and perpetually blinking, as though he had just crawled up from a deep hole.

"You mean the wood of the cross, I hope." He wavered on his feet and staggered forward a step to catch himself, so that his face was uncomfortably close to Duffy's. "Tell me you're not worshipping that tree."

"You're much too tired surely," said Duffy. "Anyway, I won't go back. Not to Nottingham. It's all heavy metal clubs and video games. Come on to see Manong and then you can rest, how about that? I'm Ted Duffy, hello." He shook hands with Graeme as they started forward through a clutch of trees.

"Please tell me," said Barney, "so we can have an idea of what's going on, if there are Christians here or if they're worshipping idols and if so where you stand." His posture improved. "I need to know if we can rely on you."

"Drawing a line in the sand? Honestly, these have been the most intriguing two minutes. Well, I think the situation in Lintek is fascinating, as an anthropological experiment if nothing else. When I came two years ago, I was horrified. Good Lord, Manong blew up a tree upon my arrival and I had to fight some poor soul to the death with a knife! Do you remember that, Kilgore?"

"Mr. Ted Duffy," said Kilgore, "fight very good." He took a knife out of his waistband and made a mighty swipe, then seemed to mime that he was picking up a head by its hair.

"It was him or me," said Duffy, holding out his arm to show them a thick scar. "Those knives are great heavy things. I'm still astounded at the thought of you strolling up here! Let me touch your hand, young lady. Good Lord!" He took Angie's hand and squeezed it.

The path was more defined now, zig-zagging up a long hill. Most of the hunters had hurried ahead of them.

"Any rate," Duffy said, "I'd been in East Africa and all the rest — famine in Ethiopia, civil war in Somalia. Managed to get out of there before the Hutus and Tutus got at it. But no, this Philippines work is altogether different. The people I used to help were sick or hungry or at least pagan. You knew where to begin, which hole to patch. Here they all had enough to eat and their idea of God wasn't so different from my own. Just much more violent."

Melissa stopped to lift her T-shirt and a half-inch beetle fell out of her navel. Graeme stepped around the beetle and bumped into Kilgore.

"But you know Manong's story?" asked Duffy. "No, of course. How could anyone? Manong actually worked on the film, you see, back in the '70s — *Apocalypse Now* — I'd seen it not long before, fortunately, with Brando in it, of course I had to see it more than once. Manong came up from Baguio, he knew his explosions, so I imagine he'd already worked on some Filipino action films, but ... things get rather cloudy around the time the film wraps up. The legend is, or he maintains, that he died of rabies during the shoot, or they thought he did, so they actually buried him …"

They were at the top of the hill, now descending. Voices shouted somewhere ahead of them. Birds flew out of the tree-tops.

"… and he rose up again. Right up out of the ground, from the dead. Of course it was rainy season and the ground was like curds and whey, so I imagine he found himself not quite dead and just swam to the surface. But they'd buried him, you see, on the last day at the location, so by the time he came up everyone had gone. The locals were extras in the film so they were still standing about wondering what to do next. It had all been rather anticlimactic until they saw our man Manong rise from the dead and walk to his room full of dynamite and start exploding things. That got their attention. Then he started in — Kurtz was hovering over everyone and all the rest of it." Duffy shrugged his shoulders and smiled at them.

"Okay, but why this Kurtz?" asked Barney. "Who is he?"

"Have you not seen the film?"

"I remember helicopters."

Graeme rolled his eyes.

"You missed Kurtz entirely?" Duffy said. "Not that he was there much, he only had about ten lines and I think they were all made up on the spot anyway. But it was Brando, wasn't it, that's the important bit. Marlon Brando, good God. This man Manong probably stood right next to him, you realize. Probably shook his hand. Now that made a real impression on me. I'm still trying to get my head around that. All of his films — *Godfather*, *On the Waterfront*, *Streetcar Named Desire* — all tremendous stories. Like a Bible if you put them together."

"Are you going to mention Christ our saviour at some point?"

"Well, I mentioned the second coming of Brando to Manong a few weeks ago, but that's not really talking about Christ, is it?" Duffy smiled ruefully. "It was an argument over whether it was Kurtz who'd return, as he insists, or my man Brando. You could easily say that they're two different names for the same entity, I know that, but you wouldn't entirely convince me."

"Insert any name you like," said Melissa.

"Kilgore, listen," said Barney. "What do you know about our Lord Jesus Christ?"

Kilgore looked at him blandly. After a moment he raised his eyebrows.

"See, *here*," said Barney, turning to Melissa, "is a place where they need us."

"Plant churches with a big shovel," she said.

"Yes!" said Barney. "Yes!"

Then Lintek was before them. A row of stone buildings was lodged into the slope facing the river, the faces of idols cut into their walls. A bizarre assortment of bamboo fences and poles tilted haphazardly in front of the buildings; weathered corpses hung from the poles.

Women sat sorting grain in the sun. A couple of sturdy men carried pots of water. Children threw sticks at a tethered dog. Chickens trotted nervously and pigs lay asleep. A dozen or more thatched huts stood around the clearing on the edge of the jungle.

"This way to Manong," said Duffy.

"Let's see what they have for us," said Barney, rubbing his hands. "Let's see, let's see."

The villagers stopped what they were doing, got up and ran in their direction: children from their games, old men from sleep, women from their looms, hunters from the skinning rack. Duffy stepped forward, as though to ward off the blow, but Barney leapt farther forward. Lintek pulled up in a semicircle around them, beads clinking, necklaces clanking. Some wore T-shirts, others tattered jeans, but otherwise it was grass skirts and woven bark. The oldest women wore sunglasses and had fragments of bone in their hair.

Melissa's elbow itched from an insect bite.

Barney raised his hands. A man in the crowd let out a hoot.

"'Blessed are the poor in spirit, for theirs is the kingdom of heaven!'" Barney paused and gave his head a shake. "'Blessed are those who mourn, for they will be comforted!'"

"Goodness, you really mean it," said Duffy.

"Let's all say it," Barney whispered to them. "Look at them! They want to hear this!"

The villagers shifted on their feet. "Willard!" yelled a young man.

"'Blessed are the meek!'" shouted Barney. "'They will inherit the Earth!'"

"Willard!" yelled a few more.

Barney turned back to Duffy. "Who is this Willard?" he asked.

"Martin Sheen is Willard, you idiot, he spends the entire film hunting Brando down so he can kill him."

"*Atoro tatataro kapok,* Willard!" they shouted.

"Does he?"

"I won't spoil it," said Duffy.

They went down a dark stone hallway, hunched under their bags, and came out in an airy room. Creepers had grown through one wall, ripping a gap several inches wide. A Filipino man with long hair and a thin moustache sat at a low table, gnawing the leg of a bird. He wore a tattered red cape and camouflage pants. A cigarette smouldered in an overturned helmet. One wall was lined with wooden boxes, stencilled with faded phrases in Filipino and English. One still clearly said DYNAMITE.

Manong glared up at them, one of his eyes cloudy and white.

"*Nay pah moaning. Nehino* Willard," Kilgore said, and indicated each of them in turn. "Willard, Willard, Willard, Willard."

Manong leaned back on his arms and scowled. He wore an old yellow T-shirt with felt lettering; it said ___*calyp__ _o_.

"You come looking for Kurtz, Willard?" said Manong. His voice was low yet painfully scratchy. "Kurtz is not here. All you many Willards come for only one Kurtz, and he is not here. Maybe you have better luck if you look for Captain Colby, played by actor Scott Glenn."

"Is Scott Glenn here?" asked Graeme.

Manong stared at him. He took a drag of his cigarette and put it back in the helmet.

"Sorry," said Duffy. He shouldered through to stand before Manong. "Is actor Scott Glenn here?"

"No, Colonel," said Manong. "I alone remain."

"And your purpose in remaining?"

"To tell about Kurtz. A very great man. But he is betrayed by his dep, dep—"

"Disciple," corrected Duffy.

"Disciple. By his disciple Willard. And is killed. Sacrificed so that we might live. Kurtz is powerful. He still walks among us." He picked out what looked like a tiny firecracker from a jar on the table, lit it off his cigarette and dropped it on the floor. It went *bang!*

"Here is Kurtz," said Manong, rolling his head back. "Everywhere Kurtz!"

Duffy turned to Melissa. "Persuasive, isn't it?"

Barney slid his duffel bag to the floor and sat cross-legged opposite Manong, who watched him wide-eyed. Barney placed his blue New Testament on the table.

"But, Manong, don't you feel," he said, his voice shaking, "that something is missing?"

Manong shot Duffy an accusing look.

"There's got to be more to it than this, don't you think?" asked Barney. "Don't you sit here sometimes and wonder what it's all for?"

"It's for Kurtz!" hollered Manong.

Duffy looked placidly down at Barney. "He finds you insubordinate."

"*Nay pah moaning,*" muttered Kilgore from the hallway.

Barney opened his mouth to speak, but instead he sneezed violently.

"Kurtz makes you sick," said Manong. "Kurtz stronger than you."

"It's the dust," said Barney. "There's no Kurtz here."

"Of course, Jesus is not here either," said Duffy. "Not that we can see."

"He's in me," said Barney. He picked up the New Testament. "He's in here."

"Kurtz is inside Manong to the same extent."

"So who's inside you?" Barney wiped his nose with his T-shirt, glaring up at Duffy. "This whole mess is based solely on a war movie and explosives, is that right?"

"Well, if Christianity is based on a dead Jew and a couple of sticks of wood, then yes. Absolutely, that's what we have."

Manong sat impassively, smoking his cigarette. A fly landed on his upper lip.

"Okay, good one. Very clever," said Barney. "But when you run out of bombs, what's left of the religion? They all go back to what they were doing before, thanking the god of pigs for their harvest or whatever they used to do?"

"Oh, it's all interchangeable," said Duffy. "We want reassurance that we have a place in this world. We want to know that no matter how repulsive our lives, something or someone has an interest in us. That the god of pigs *cares*."

Manong rose, picked up a wooden crate and dropped it on the table, spilling the helmet of ashes into Barney's lap. Melissa backed away, Graeme and Angie crowding in next to her.

"Kurtz is here!" howled Manong and he threw off the lid and pulled out a faded purple stick with a fuse in the end. He struck a match and lit it, thrusting the dynamite into Barney's face. Barney gripped his Bible. "Kurtz is here!" Manong screamed, the fuse burning greedily.

Barney leapt to his feet, seized the stick of dynamite, threw it through the crack in the wall and dove for cover. Manong stood transfixed. Melissa pulled Graeme and Angie down beside her. She was ready for leaves and shards of wood to fly in through the windows.

They waited half a minute.

"Powder must be off in that one," said Duffy. He took a stick from the box and smelled it. "Oh, they're mouldy. Whole box is off."

"No," said Graeme, "I guess I don't know what you want."

"Just tell them how you feel about Christ," said Barney. He had his shirt off and his chest hairs were speckled with white. He dropped the little dog and got to his feet.

"How do you know I feel anything?" asked Graeme.

A village girl in blue shorts scooped the dog up and nuzzled it under her chin, covering her bare breasts with its body. The noon heat justified her nakedness, Melissa thought. She remembered the nude beach at home — this time of year it would only be the Fairbridge brothers and a couple of other stalwarts.

"Well, don't you?" asked Barney.

"Look, I'll talk to them when I feel like it."

"Do I have to convince you?" said Barney. "Is that what's going on?"

"Did you ever ask him about it?" asked Angie. She sat beside Graeme in her bra, her dreadlocks on her tanned shoulders.

"What?" asked Barney.

"It's not a crazy question. I'm curious if you asked Graeme if he believed in anything before you brought him out here."

"He believes in God," said Barney, "as strongly as I do. And, Graeme, call me a liar if you want to, but I doubt if you've got the balls to do that to my face."

"Why are you freaking out?" said Graeme.

"Just talk to those kids! They're sitting right there!"

The topless girl frowned and twisted her shoulders as she danced with the dog. It licked her chin. Five boys sat in the dirt behind her, building tiny walls and paths out of rocks and sticks. As far as Melissa could tell the big green rock was Kurtz and it walked up and down with impunity.

"I don't see what the hurry is," Melissa said. "Let them get used to us, if that's how Harry Egan did it. He took six months."

Barney smirked and sat back down on the log. "Theodore Duffy took his time, too, and look how far that got him."

"Look, Dad," said Graeme. "Angie and I were thinking we might hike around a bit, get to see the country."

"What, for the day?"

"For a few days maybe."

Barney picked a leaf and seemed to weigh it in his hand. He pulled at his moustache with his lower lip. "Sounds fine. Go," he said, "but this is what I was put on Earth to do." He looked at the three of them. "Maybe I'm not very good at it. But we'll see. We'll see. I'm going to sing to these people and they're going to gather around. I will give *everything* I have." He shut his eyes. "If you're not with me then I say get the hell out of here." He tore the leaf in half.

They sat there in the sun as though nothing had been said. Melissa couldn't tell how long that moment lasted, the girl dancing in circling steps, but eventually Graeme pulled the camouflage jacket over his shoulders and rolled up the sleeves. He got to his feet. Barney sighed and stood up too. They were only a few feet apart.

"So we should go," said Graeme.

Melissa watched as Barney's face worked to regain composure, or any expression at all. His hands became fists.

"Graeme," said Angie, "just walk away from him."

"It's all right," said Barney. He looked at Melissa, then back at Graeme. His hands relaxed. "I brought you up here. But, Graeme, it's your choice what happens now. You see what needs to be done. These people are doomed without us. If you can turn your back on that, if you are still truly that *ignorant*, then nothing I say or do can change you. You should get on."

Graeme turned and walked away. He went past the huts and out of sight.

"Nice speech," said Angie. She stood and brushed off her shorts.

Barney said nothing.

Inside the hut the space around the fire was filled with the bent brown legs of the men in loincloths, the fire casting an orange glow on their knees. They were restless, a few clearly saying "Willard" and pointing shaky fingers at Melissa and Barney sitting beside the cooking pot. Duffy squatted beside them in a torn CWF windbreaker, nibbling on a cooked banana.

With a clang one man struck a large knife against a stone.

Lance leaned in front of him, the flames reflecting in the long teeth of his necklace, and spoke in soothing tones while the man patted the blade against the palm of his hand. Men chewing twists of root spat toward the fire and twice hit Barney on the foot.

An old man with a patchy white beard leapt to his feet and Melissa felt Barney quiver beside her. "Willard!" the man screamed. "Willard!" He swept the wing of a chicken over their heads, then with some glee opened his hand to reveal what looked like the chicken's guts. "*Atoro tatataro kapok!*"

"I was keen to martyr myself when I first arrived," Duffy said into her ear. "But I cooled to the idea when I realized that not a soul would appreciate it. They bury you in a clearing. You don't benefit anyone that way." He looked at her meaningfully, got to his feet and moved around the fire toward the door.

"*Nangarohi larahnangow!*" White Beard took a string of entrails and threw it onto Barney's shoulder. Black smoke gusted in their faces.

"*Kivi maowa!*" Teeth gnashed.

"I'm not going to do anything," Barney said quietly.

Now more men clustered around the door, blocking any exit. "*Elamo dasaho lutan!*" Someone punched her leg, hard.

"'Consider him who endured such opposition from sinful men,'" said Barney, "'so that you will not grow weary and lose heart.' Hebrews 12:1."

Another piece of meat hit him in the neck. The old man leapt in the air.

"Barney," said Melissa.

A figure shuffled through the door, his face blocked by shadow until he pushed against the old man and stood astride the fire. It was Manong, wearing a loincloth.

"Kurtz," someone said.

Manong was sweaty and shaking, his eyes rolled back in his

head. He stamped one foot, then the other. On his head he wore what looked like a wicker lampshade with a plume in the side, but he threw it on the flames. He rubbed his head with the flat of his hand as the heat licked his calves. The moaning continued, trying to fight its way out of him, his head lurching back and forth.

"We ... must incinerate them." It was not Manong's own voice. "Pig ... after pig."

The men crouched around Manong, their knees in the flames, groping for his hand and arm, some of them whimpering. The old man embraced Manong around the waist. The men moaned, rubbing their heads, whispering "Kurtz" to each other, the holy name resplendent on their tongues. Shadows flashed in blurred patterns across the ceiling, flames hovering over their heads.

Manong staggered over the fire, ash clouding around his knees. He seemed to search for something through his blindness. His hands caressed the air. After a moment he grasped either side of Barney's head. The moan bubbled out of him.

"If I ... were to be killed ... Willard." The men gathered in, White Beard kneeling beside Barney. A rope of drool hung from Manong's chin and his hands tightened around Barney's temples, twisting his head sideways. "I want someone ... to tell my son ... everything." Whose voice was it? Manong's accent was not there — good Lord, was it Marlon Brando?

"Willard, you will do this for me."

Manong's eyes snapped open and he would have fallen back into the fire but for the hands already on him. He wiped his mouth. He took a pipe from someone and started puffing away. The cook righted his iron pot.

The men crouched to study Barney. Manong wandered outside.

White Beard put a hand on Barney's knee, looking deep into his eyes. Then he moved to sit with the other men and they whispered to each other, nodding earnestly.

Barney leaned forward to stretch his back, then looked at Melissa. "'Discipline seems painful,'" he said, "'though it produces a harvest of righteousness.'"

Barney woke her up. It was cold in the mountains at night. She had two towels and a blanket over her and even in the dark she could see his breath.

"What was it?" he asked. "What was it Harry always said or said that one time when we said we'd do this? You have to grab God, something like that? Do you remember how we were supposed to grab him?"

"With our fists." Sleep was holding down her tongue. "In our fists."

"Grab God with both fists!" He gave her shoulder a squeeze and ran out of the hut. After a minute she heard his feet running across a patch of gravel. Then only the sound of insects.

She sat in the doorway and looked out, the blanket over her shoulders. There was still no moon, but a mass of stars hovered in the sky. She could make out some of the huts and guess where Manong's buildings were, where fewer treetops stood against the horizon.

The insects' whirring changed keys. She shivered.

It dawned on her how random all of this was. The notion of God flickered through her head, or Fate, or some power that wove the world into its fabric, deciding painstakingly where each thread would fall. Just as quickly she discarded that notion, though, because it was *Barney* who had decided that she would look out at this night, Barney and no one else. Where others could look to some higher power she had only to look to him. But she had chosen Barney for herself. No one could argue with that.

Graeme and Angie had been gone for less than a day; they were going down to the coast to go surfing. Melissa had given him half of her money. They would all meet again in Tinapa.

She lay down on her mat, curling into a ball for warmth. She put one of the towels around her feet and waited until she was warm enough to drift off.

Insects buzzed, contented and low. The river murmured its farewells to the huts and creepers and bats hanging in trees as it started for the South China Sea.

She was at the peak of the world now, resting at the plateau. She could descend in any direction.

The phone office in Baguio was nearly empty. Melissa stood in the middle booth while the attendant sat beside the front door.

The receiver buzzed monotonously, then clicked several times. She leaned against the cool metal of the booth and watched the traffic move past the office window. Two men sauntered past, carrying a pig impaled lengthwise on a pole. John had told her there was a festival on, but she couldn't remember what it was for.

Finally it began to ring: a clean, healthy, Canadian ring. It was four in the afternoon for her, so that meant midnight of the day before in Vancouver.

"Hello?"

"Hello, is that Bob? It's Melissa Jordan. In the Philippines."

"Mrs. Jordan?"

"Thought I'd better call to let everyone know we're okay. How are you?"

"Oh, well, Rita and I are fine, of course, but Melissa, we were concerned. Thought we'd never hear from you. Have you been sick?"

"Well, we had trouble in Manila. Apparently they didn't know we were coming. But since then it's been clear sailing."

"Is that right? Well, I told Barney he had to let them know you'd be coming, but of course he had to do it off the cuff."

"Like Indiana Jones, he says."

"That's right, is that what he says? I'll tell that to Harry. How's everything else? How is Graeme finding it?"

"It's been good for him. He's met a girlfriend here—"

"I can't imagine Barney—"

"That's just it, you know. Graeme's grown up now and he's got to do the work of, of Jesus too. That's what we're here for."

"Now where have you ended up? One of Harry's boys was making noise about heading over there."

"Well, there are so many little places here, Bob—"

"And the Parks Board was trying to get a hold of Barney about a job, but I went and told them he already had one. They had to — Oh, Rita wants me to ask you about Mr. Thomas, after all the stories — maybe you'd like to speak to her?"

"You tell her he's terrific. I'd better get moving, we're just here picking up supplies. I think Barney wanted you to know how well we were getting on."

"It sounds very exciting, Melissa. How many souls, can I ask you that? Have you kept count?"

She watched John cross the street. Some men were loading rice into the back of the truck. John picked up a box of potatoes.

"Oh, Bob, we've lost count. We really have."

"Well, we'll give your mother a call and let her know how you are. We expected a call a few weeks ago."

"We should get moving, I'm afraid."

"All right, then, take care. God bless you."

"Okay. Goodbye."

She hung up the receiver and stepped out of the booth. The attendant was drawing up the bill.

AKNOWLEDGEMENTS

Thanks to the publications in which the following stories appeared: "Pak Arafim the Pharmacist," *The Malahat Review*; "Kingdom of Monkeys," *Zygote*; "Balinese," *Best Canadian Stories* (anthology), Oberon Press; "Distance" as "The Distance between Prague and New Orleans," *Scribner's Best of the Fiction Workshops* (anthology), Simon & Schuster.

Thanks to Kelli Deeth, Derek Fairbridge, Jasmine MacAdam, Rick Maddocks and Linda Svendsen — the stories' first readers — for their invaluable advice.

Thanks to everyone at Hostelling International BC Region, UBC Creative Writing, A Western Theatre Conspiracy and Arse Kick Productions.

Thanks to travellers near and far — Les Bergman, Yance de Fretes, Chad Hackman, Nicole Handford and Kerri Thompson among them.

Thanks to Amber J. Lin.

Thanks to the Advents, Handfords, Schroeders and Suttons.

The excerpt from *The Sheltering Sky* by Paul Bowles (Vintage, 1990), *Don't Fence Me In* by Cole Porter (Harms, 1944) and dialogue from *Apocalypse Now* (United Artists/Zoetrope, 1979) are used with permission.

More Raincoast Fiction:

Slow Lightning by Mark Frutkin
1–55192–406–4 $21.95 CDN/$16.95 US

In 1936 civil war Spain Sandro Risco Canovas is blacklisted by Franco and forced to flee the city, posing as a priest along the sacred pilgrimage route, the Saint James Way. Sandro makes his way to a secret cave near his seaside home of Arcasella, setting in motion an elaborate deception that signals a descent into darkness, dream and desire.

After Battersea Park by Jonathan Bennett
1-55192-408-0 $21.95 CDN/$16.95 US

In a twist on the twins-separated-at-birth story Australian Canadian Jonathan Bennett pens a tale of 27-year-old brothers drawn toward a reunion when a suicide note reveals the identity of their true parents. In a chase that spans three continents, the estranged sons unravel the wrenching events of London's Battersea Park twenty-three years earlier.

Finnie Walsh by Steven Galloway
1-55192-377-6 $21.95 CDN/$16.95 US

Finnie Walsh is Paul Woodward's best friend, a hockey fanatic and the tragic figure at the heart of a series of bizarre accidents that alter the lives of the Woodward family in a comic tale of family, friendship, redemption and legend.

Hotel Paradiso by Gregor Robinson
1–55192-358–0 $21.95 CDN/$16.95 US

Journey Prize nominee Gregor Robinson's debut novel charts a season in the life of a thirty-something expat banker in the Bahamian out-port of Pigeon Cay. He has come to the subtropics in search of exotic escape, but instead stumbles upon genteel corruption, white collar crime, racism and murder.

Rhymes with Useless by Terence Young
1-55192-354-8 $18.95 CDN/$14.95 US

In a collection praised by *The Village Voice*, *Publisher's Weekly*, *National Post* and the *Globe & Mail*, Governor General's nominee Terence Young creates both a litany of human foibles and its sensible antidote; regret and forgiveness, suppressed desire and unleashed lust, dislocation and homecoming.

Song of Ascent by Gabriella Goliger
1-55192-374-2 $18.95 CDN/$14.95 US

Journey Prize winner Gabriella Goliger's finely-honed stories recount the troubled lives of the Birnbaum family, displaced German Jews who flee Hitler but cannot escape the shadow of the Holocaust. Their uprooted existence takes them from Europe to the Holy Land to Montreal to relate a history that explores the tense dialogue between present and past.